LOVE
OBSESSED

LOVE

OBSESSED

a novel

by

BRUCE K BECK

AUDACITY BOOKS
WE DARE TO TELL THE TRUTH

New York

This book is dedicated to all lovers. Without us, the world would still turn. But really, what would be the point?

Chapter One

I suppose my parents loved me. Mother said
she did, a time or two. Dad? Not really. But he had
a certain warmth about him. I didn't question our
relationships—while everyone was living. But I see
young families these days—on the street and in
shops and restaurants—and they seem so easy with
their affection. That was not *my* childhood.

I wouldn't have been thinking about my parents
at all if I hadn't noticed a young father playing a ball
game with his son while I was walking through Central Park one glorious afternoon last fall. The kid
lobbed an impressive throw that went over his father's head and right into my arms. I'm not much of
a catcher, but I managed to hold onto the ball—to
my surprise. And I was also surprised at the warmth
of the father's smile as he apologized for my inconvenience and retrieved the toy.

"Will Granger," he said, as he extended his hand.

"Oliver Hartmann," I said, as I shook it.

"Good catch!" he said.

"Lucky, I think," I said.

"It's a beautiful afternoon, but I think Sam and I
have had enough. I promised him a hot chocolate.
Will you join us?"

"Sure," I said. We were quite near my apartment,
and there was nothing waiting for me on my desk

that I really wanted to tackle. So instead I joined Will and Sam at a little neighborhood place on Columbus Avenue. I decided on a glass of wine instead of hot chocolate. But I almost regretted my decision when the waitress brought the father and son their steamy brews. It was fun, being with them. They obviously adored each other. And I must say they were both adorable. "I don't think I've ever seen the park look better than it does this fall," I said.

"No," Will said. "The leaves are perfect this year. I'm glad Sam's school gave him a few days off."

"*You're* glad," Sam said.

Will reached out and tousled his son's hair. "Okay, Sammy. Let's get you home. Nora said dinner will be early tonight. Say goodbye to Mr. Hartmann." Sam shook my hand. "Here's my phone number," Will said to me. "Could I call you some time?"

"Of course," I said as we exchanged numbers. And I hoped he would. Will was great looking: tall and slim with a terrific smile and an easy grace about him. But I've made it a rule not to get involved with straight men. I mean, really, what's the point? Relationships are difficult enough when both parties are on the same page. And a relationship was what I most needed at the time. Or so I thought.

"It was good to meet you, Oliver," Will said. "I'll call you soon." And they were off. I finished my wine and then strolled home. I love my apartment. I bought it right after college with much of what was left in my trust fund. It's in one of those generous old buildings on Central Park West. Beautiful wood floors, high ceilings, a kitchen that was last modernized in the seventies, creaky old plumbing, and very expensive air conditioning in the summer.

It's technically a one-bedroom apartment, but there's another, smaller room in the back with its own bathroom. Intended as maid's quarters, of course. My bedroom and the living room share the same view of Central Park. It's not a high floor—the twelfth, only—but it gives me a sense of being perched above the city. I set up my desk right by the bedroom window. Whenever I'm working, I get to look up from my laptop screen and out onto one of the most glorious public spaces in the world.

The seasons parade before my eyes. The morning sunlight is different every day, filtered by the weather and the colors in the park. I get to experience the rosy shimmer of sunset, as it settles over the city, and the sparkle of starry nights. Even at my darkest times I've been able to find a sense of gratitude for what I have. Well, most of my darkest times, anyway.

My innate optimism was sorely tested by my last breakup. I thought Carlos was perfect. And—to be fair—I should say that he was *close* to perfection. He was handsome, he was charming, he was smart, he was interested in theater and museums and the opera and good food and drink. He was interested in me. And he had a dick the Devil would envy. I thought we were in it for the long haul. I thought we had achieved a level of intimacy that would sustain us—and isn't that everything, after all?

I can't tell you that Carlos stole things or turned out to be a con artist. It wasn't like that. Perhaps it might have been easier to accept if he had been some awful fraud. Instead, he simply lost interest in me—in us—over time. It was so gradual that I barely saw it coming. That's not entirely true, of course. Mates know. But whatever I actually knew about what was happening, I was still blindsided by the reality that it was over. I said to him, "Carly, I love you. Why isn't that enough?"

"I don't know, Ollie," he said. "I wish it were. I love you, too. But I can't do this anymore." When Carlos left me, did I consider hurling myself out my window and onto the sidewalk below? No. That never occurred to me, fortunately. But my life came to an abrupt standstill that lasted for weeks. It was work that forced me to function again. Deadlines. I'm a writer—copy for ads and magazines plus the occasional ghostwritten memoir or novel. Actually, I don't differentiate between the two. It's all fiction, I think.

My oldest friend, Jerry Weintraub, phoned me every day, as always. That was the only semblance of normality in my period of mourning. But one day I had had enough of dormancy. I came out of my cocoon and started participating in life again. Did I emerge transformed? No beautiful butterfly, I. More like a moth, I think. Jerry took me to dinner or pushed me to go to a concert. I always loved dance. ABT was in season at the Met Opera House—a nice walk from my apartment. I got tickets. I was living again.

That was the mode I was in that beautiful fall afternoon when I met Will Granger. I felt alive but alone. Could Will maybe help me change that? The alone part? I suspected not. But I didn't rule it out.

📖

"Hi, Oliver. It's Will Granger." I answered the phone because I recognized his number.

"Hi, Will. You said you'd call."

"Yes. I was wondering if you'll have dinner with me on Friday."

"Sure," I said. "That sounds nice."

"Sam is going to spend the weekend with his mother—in Boston. I'll confess I get really lonely when he's away, so I could use some company."

I was flattered that Will turned to me for companionship. But I also felt a twinge of sadness that I would be merely a stand-in for his son—his real life. "What were you thinking about—for dinner?" I asked.

"Why don't we meet at the new Italian restaurant on 74th—I think it is—between Columbus and Amsterdam? I'll double check it and text you the address. I'm on West End Avenue, so it's about halfway between us."

"Sounds good," I said.

"7:00?"

"Perfect,"

"Good," he said. "I'm looking forward to seeing you again."

"Yes. So am I," I said. *Holy shit!* I thought. *What am I getting myself into?* I didn't really dwell on it. I had work to do. My big project was an "autobiography" for a movie star whose career dried up decades ago. He moved to New York at about the same time, and he rarely works these days. But he does hold court in neighborhood businesses—the pharmacy, the fish market, the gourmet shop. I've gone out with him on his rounds a few times, and he seems to love the interaction. The shop owners know him, of course. I'd estimate at least half the customers have no idea who the effusive older man is. But he continues to try to charm people, and he succeeds more often than not.

The book helped me keep my mind off Will. There was no point in my creating an elaborate romantic fantasy. No point at all. It was dinner at a nearby restaurant, nothing more. True? Probably. It didn't matter, but I got a little nervous anyway, as Friday approached. I dressed with care, choosing cords and a butter-colored, light-weight cashmere pullover. I looked good. I grabbed my jacket and headed out.

"Right on time," Will said as he greeted me at the bar.

"Nice place," I said. "I hadn't noticed it, so I think they must have just opened."

"In September, I think," Will said. "I walk this block often, so I kind of watched it come together." The hostess seated us at a comfortable table. The menu looked interesting. We decided to share a pasta, to start, followed by veal—with mushrooms for Will and artichoke hearts for me, I think. The wine was overpriced, of course, but then where isn't it these days? And when we had ordered, I could relax and enjoy the company.

"Will, I know nothing about you, except that you have an exceptionally good-looking son," I said. "The apple doesn't fall far from the tree. But I'll bet there's more to you than that."

"Sam is a cutie, isn't he?" Will said. "I'm an architect. I took my apartment—before Sam was born—because I liked the look of the building. My wife, Jennifer, and I were happy there, or so I thought. But she bolted when Sam was nearly four. You don't want to hear the details. Sam didn't fit with her new life, so he's been with me all along. I found a live-in housekeeper. Nora's been with us almost five years now. Without her, I couldn't go to work every day and concentrate. But she's part of our family, thank God. I think that's enough of my history for one dinner."

"Thanks, Will," I said. "I think you're very brave. My story is quite different. I'm a writer. You've probably read a few of my books, but with someone else's name on the cover. Maybe I'll write one with *my* name on the cover. Perhaps next year. Who knows? I'm single, these days. But not by choice. I'm gay, of course, but then you knew that. My last partner, Carlos, left me less than a year ago. I wish we had known each other then. We could have commiserated about what to do when a spouse flees."

"It isn't pretty, is it?" Will asked. "I had Sam to consider, so I didn't have much time for grief. I still don't. Sometimes I wonder if I'll ever get past it. Probably not. It's become part of who I am. And you?"

"I tried to white-knuckle it. I was in deep denial for weeks," I said. "But one day I just said, 'Fuck it! I want to live.' And that's what I've been doing ever since."

"Good for you, Oliver! I took you for a survivor," Will said. "And a very handsome survivor at that."

"Will, are you flirting with me?" I asked.

"I'm glad you recognized it," he said. "It's so long since I had a romantic feeling that I'm not sure I know how to act on it."

"This is getting interesting, but really, Will, what's going on?"

"Other than two men sharing a good dinner?"

"Other than two men sharing a good dinner," I said.

"Oliver, could I get right to the point?

"Please do," I said.

"I feel I know you, Oliver. And I also feel I need to make love to you. If you'll consider me. Will you come to my apartment? Nora's visiting her sister in New Jersey while Sam's away. I haven't had another man in my bed since—since college, really. Will you help me change that?"

"Jesus, Will!" I said. " 'Wanna fuck?' would have been sufficient. You don't have to woo me. But I'm touched that you did. Of course I'll join you. In fact, I'm thinking maybe we should skip coffee and go now. What do you think?"

"I think you're absolutely right. Let's get a check." And that's what we did. There was urgency in our walk to West End. There was also the giddy pleasure of newness and promise. We didn't talk much. We smiled a lot. We held hands—briefly, at one point. But as we neared Will's building we adopted more sober decorum. Why shouldn't the handsome young architect have a man visit his apartment? Business, probably. I watched that posing when I was in college. I hadn't really seen it since. I felt slightly put off by the pretense. I also felt deeply attracted to Will Granger.

Chapter Two

I've never really had a "type," I think. I respond to quality maleness. The particulars of the packaging are almost irrelevant. Carlos, for instance, was medium height, dark hair, tightly muscled, with a bubble butt and—I already told you about his equipment. I signed on for the duration. I would have honored him for the rest of my life, if he had valued me. Will, on the other hand, was long and lean—willowy, almost. He was not blonde—like his son—but fair, certainly. And I was more than willing. Ready? Yes. Eager, I think, is how to describe my reaction to Will.

His apartment was gorgeous. Spare, but deeply comfortable. A little Mies, a little Breuer, a little Wiener Werkstätte. A little Mexican Modernism. It all worked perfectly. He welcomed me. "Will you have maybe a whiskey, or something?" he asked.

"Sure, whatever you're having." Will brought us Scotches—single malt, I think—with a splash of water and one ice cube. It was delicious. I sipped. I waited.

"Would you like to talk, or maybe go to my bedroom?" Will asked.

"Both," I said. "Bedroom first, please."

"Yes, that was my thought, too," he said. I followed him to his room. "I don't remember how to do this," Will said.

"You don't have to *do* anything," I said. "Except kiss me. That's a requisite." He did, of course. Will's kiss was warm and open, like his nature. We began to undress. And when we finally faced each other in full birthday, I asked, "What do you think?"

"I think you're beautiful, Oliver. And I think I'm going to cry."

"It's allowed," I said. "I may join you." Will's body was even more toned and supple than I had imagined. I asked him to lie back and let me explore it. He did. There was a lot to like, from his ears to his elegant toes and all parts in between. I had a good trip. Will gave me the onceover, too. When we had gotten to know each other's bodies a little, then we got more serious about finding ways to hold each other close.

Will said, "Oliver, I want . . . I want you on top." I kissed Will deeply. I caressed him warmly. I began to move my body into position. I was ready. But I sensed that Will was not. Ready. He seemed tense. Tightly wound. He seemed eager but apprehensive. I didn't want to hurt him. I didn't want our first lovemaking to be anything but pleasurable. I didn't want to try something that could go wrong.

"Could we save that for next time?" I asked. "When it's not so late and we haven't had a huge dinner."

"Of course, Oliver," he said, and he held me tightly. He seemed relieved. We found other things to do, of course. Eventually I focused on his long, lean dick, which was delicious. I had a really good time with his generous foreskin. I wondered how

Will, the perfect WASP, had escaped the scalpel. Carlos did, too, but of course Latins aren't big on cutting. I didn't spend long speculating why Will was gloriously intact. I simply savored him.

I could tell that Will was getting close, so I edged him—to delay the inevitable end to our sweet little drama. But when there was no holding back, Will erupted with great surges of hot, white jism. I greedily consumed it all. "Jesus, Will, what a shot!" I said. "You must have been saving that up for weeks."

He looked a little sheepish. He said, "The truth is, I masturbate often. Usually every night. It's my only release. But this week, I thought, *No, I want to save this for Oliver. Just in case. He deserves my best.* Does that make me a pervert?"

"No, it makes you an exceptionally sweet man," I said. "And you notice I savored every drop. You could become my new favorite dessert."

"You're already my new favorite *friend*," Will said. "I don't want to sound needy, although clearly I am. I don't have much in the way of friendship in my life these days. Oliver, do you think we could be friends?"

"We already are, Will," I said. "And our friendship can only deepen. It really is late. I'm going to head home."

"I hoped you'd sleep over," he said.

"I'm flattered that you asked," I said, "but I can't see it—a man sleeping over in the handsome young architect's apartment while his son and his housekeeper are away. I don't think that would work in your building. I wouldn't do that to you. You could come in or out of my building at all hours of the day or night—and I hope you will—and no one would raise an eyebrow. They all know who I am. But here? No," I said as I dressed. "I'm going to take off. Will, can I see you—tomorrow and Sunday? I haven't made any weekend plans. I'd like nothing more than for you to come and stay with me."

"Oliver, now you really will make me cry. Yes! I'll come. I have some work to do at my desk in the morning. But I'll be there as close to noon as possible. What should I bring?"

"Don't be silly. You don't need to bring a thing," I said. "We can order in food when we need it, and I have plenty of wine in the house. And some spirits. I have an extra toothbrush and an extra razor. Whatever you're wearing when you arrive on Saturday should look just fine when you wear it home on Sunday. I don't intend for you to wear much of anything while you're with me."

"I'll stop on my way over and get something for our lunch. I don't really know what you like."

"Besides you?"

"Besides me."

"This weekend, I like anything you like. And after that? We'll talk."

"Thanks, Oliver," he said. Will walked me to the door. We shared a dreamy kiss, and then I headed out into the night. *What the fuck!* I thought as I strolled home. *I went to dinner and left with a house guest.* My invitation caught me off guard. But I issued it because I wanted very much to spend time with Will Granger, after all. And he clearly wanted to spend time with me. It would be fine. It would be better than fine. It would be delicious. Wouldn't it?

Chapter Three

It was close to 1:00 when Will arrived at my apartment. I had already phoned down to tell the doorman to send him right up. He was carrying two takeout bags and a small bouquet of flowers. I had already set the dining table for our luncheon. I had a vase for Will's flowers. I had a vase for every occasion, thanks to my mother. I placed Will's posies in the chosen vessel and added them to the table. Then I could focus on their bearer. I embraced Will as tenderly as I dared. I kissed him deeply. He responded totally. "If lunch is as tasty as that kiss, then our weekend is definitely off to a great start," I said.

"Agreed," Will said. "Shall we eat something?"

"Sure," I said. "I had almost no breakfast at all, so I'm famished." That was the truth. I had been a little nervous about hosting. I straightened the apartment a bit. Betina only came in to clean every other week those days, but she had been in recently, so the kitchen and bathroom were in good shape. I popped out to the Sturgeon King for some smoked salmon for Sunday breakfast. And a lemon. I had everything else in the house—bread for toasting, cream cheese, capers, a red onion, a couple of ripe plum tomatoes. The rest of our meals we could improvise. I was prepared.

Will followed me to the kitchen, where we un-packed his luncheon goodies. He brought falafels, hummus, and baba ganoush, and a wonderful big salad. "Don't eat too much!" I admonished him.

"I wouldn't think of it," he said. I loved watching Will enjoy his lunch. He was so elegant, even when chewing. We smiled at each other a lot. We took our time. We lingered at the table over coffee. I had an-other glass of wine. And then we headed to my bed.

It was a treat to explore Will's body in daylight. His shoulders and chest were surprisingly strong, and his limbs well-turned. Tennis, no doubt. I'm a big fan of armpits, so I spent some quality time there. I worked my way down. By the time I got to Will's crotch, I was ready to enjoy its totality. Imagine that you were guessing at Will's equipment based on see-ing him in street clothes. Your best-case scenario would have turned out to be the reality.

Will's dick was long and lean, like his body. That I was already aware of from the night before. What I had missed in the low light of his bedroom was the exquisite beauty of his balls. I have a devotion to balls, I'll admit. But they are considered, after all—even in polite society—to be the seat of masculinity. They certainly are for me. Will's balls were large and perfectly matched. They hung low enough to be to-tally available, for play or worship. They never seemed to hide. Will offered them to me with the same generosity as he offered all his gifts. I received them with reverence.

I rolled Will over and straddled his back so I could massage his strong shoulders. I worked my way down. By the time I got to his dimples, I knew I would become a devoté. Will's butt was lean and muscled, like the rest of him, with just enough cushioning to make me feel welcome. I took the plunge and buried my face between his legs. Will moaned as my tongue found the sweet spot. I could have stayed there for hours. Will seemed content with the arrangement. But we had other activities ahead.

I rolled him back over. For the first union of our bodies, I wanted Will on his back—so I could see his face at all times and kiss him easily and naturally as often as I wanted, which would turn out to be very often indeed. That time Will was ready. We placed his lean, strong legs on my shoulders. I caressed them as I presented my dick—carefully, gently. I studied Will's face intently. He smiled sweetly. He also grabbed my thighs and pulled me to him. Will gasped. I was in. "Are you okay?" I asked.

"Perfect," he said. His smile soon returned. I loved Will's sex face. He looked positively angelic as he received me. I leaned forward to kiss him, and he wrapped his arms around my torso. I had never felt so close to another human as I did while Will and I bonded our bodies for the first time. We seemed to touch at all points. What had been two bodies before our merger became one. It was bliss.

I resisted the urge to speed up, as I got closer. But Will knew, of course, by my breathing. He reached for my thighs and encouraged me to stay deep. He was still gripping me when I shouted, "Jesus Christ," and let go. He gave me a moment to recover before he said, "Stay with me." I reached for Will's dick, and after maybe two strokes he let loose, too. Will's orgasm was a beautiful thing to experience. And I got to share it inside and out.

Many men have one or two good shots followed by dribble. Will didn't hit zenith until his fourth spasm. The third shot reached his chest; the fourth, his glorious Adam's apple; the fifth, his chest again; and after that, diminishing range. I stayed very still so I could feel each pulse as well as see the result. I lost count after the twelfth. It was remarkable. It was beautiful. I felt blessed that he shared it with me. I felt proud that I had encouraged that lovely event.

That time I shared the bounty with Will. I wondered if he had ever tasted his own semen. Perhaps not. His natural modesty might have kept him from exploring what he produced. But he seemed to like it. Perhaps not as much as I did, but then it's beyond tasting for me—it's sacrament.

I got some robes for us, and we headed for the kitchen. We sat. I poured some chardonnay. Will wanted to phone Sam. "Hi, Sammy, how are you? . . . Good. What are you up to? . . . That sounds like fun. I had lunch with Mr. Hartmann. . . . Yes, he *is* a nice guy. I'll tell him you said hello. . . . I love you, too, Sammy. Enjoy yourself, and I'll see you tomorrow night." When Will finished his phone call, he sat quietly for a minute. He looked—concerned, I suppose. He said, "I miss Sam when he goes to visit his mother, but I also worry about him. Because he loves her so much, and he's always excited about seeing her. But when he gets home, he's always depressed for a few days. I don't know if it's leaving her or leaving home or whether he relives the day she abandoned us. Maybe some of each."

"He's a good kid, Will," I said. "He'll be fine."

"I'm sure you're right," he said. "What should we do this afternoon? We can't make love all the time, can we?"

"Let's pace ourselves," I suggested. "I think we have time to see a movie before I get hungry again."

"Hungry for dinner, or for me?"

"Both, I expect. What would you like to see?" We chose a romcom and settled on the sofa to watch it. I didn't really use the living room very often. But it had a larger screen than the bedroom did. And the sofa was very comfortable. I snuggled up against Will, and he put his arms around me. I felt warm. I felt safe. The picture was okay, I suppose. It was difficult for me to focus on anything other than the Will Granger Show. I found that riveting.

After the movie we returned to my bed for another chance to bond. That one was mostly about kisses. I never could get my fill of those. And then it was time to think about dinner. "How about Thai?" I asked.

"Sure," Will said. "Whatever you like." I ordered some food from a place on Amsterdam. I probably ordered too many dishes, but I was only just learning about Will's appetite. I didn't want him to feel that I hadn't offered him enough. We set the table. The delivery arrived. We ate. We talked. We straightened up, and then we returned to my bed. We held each other for a while.

"What's going on here, Will?" I asked.

"I'm falling in love with you, Oliver. That's all I can tell you."

"I was afraid of something like that," I said. "I've always steered clear of [I didn't say *straight* men] family men. I require full-time care and feeding. I don't know how I'd learn to share you. But I want you, Will. I'm falling in love with you, too. No surprise there, I'm sure."

"What are we going to do about this?" Will asked.

"Other than being very good to each other?"

"Other than being very good to each other."

"I don't know," I said. "But, fortunately, we don't have to make any decisions like that for, maybe, twenty-four hours. Will you just stay here in my bed?"

"Of course," Will said. And that's what we did. I wasn't certain I'd be able to sleep that night. I didn't want to miss a moment of Will—beside me in my bed, with our arms entwined. His breath warmed my chest. Eventually Will's breathing became even and automatic, and I knew that sleep had claimed him. I soon joined him.

Waking in the morning with Will beside me in my bed was joyous. He was so beautiful, with his sleep-tousled hair and his angelic smile. My heart gave a little leap at the sheer wonder of it all. We put on robes and headed for the kitchen. We set up our breakfast on the kitchen table. It was a slow process, what with all the pauses for kisses. But there was no rush, after all. We ate. We lingered over breakfast coffee.

"What shall we do today?" I asked.

"Besides making love?" he asked.

"Besides making love."

"How about a walk in the park? I think we're going to get good weather."

"Only if we can return to the scene of our first meeting," I said.

"Naturally," Will said. "I'm sentimental, too." And that's what we did. We started by taking a leisurely shower together. It was a treat for me, like everything I did with Will. Afterward, we dried off and kissed some more.

"No deodorant, please," I said. I was planning ahead for our afternoon session in my bed.

"As you desire me," Will said. I gave him some shorts and a pair of my jeans I figured would be long enough for him if we rolled down the cuffs. They were fine. I gave him a sweater. We put on our jackets and headed out. The park was magical, as always. And we did score some fine weather. We walked for hours, often arm in arm.

"Tell me more about you," I said. "For instance, how did you manage to escape circumcision?"

"Oh, that's easy. My mother's English, and she couldn't see the point in it. So she said, 'No,' and Dad didn't get involved. I grew up in Connecticut. Did I tell you that? And I went to Yale. And then I got a job with a New York City firm. It was an apprenticeship to start. But then it became a real job, and I've been there ever since. Oliver, I know next to nothing about you."

"There isn't much I like to talk about, but I'll give it a try. I grew up in Westchester, which was pleasant enough when I was little, but I grew to hate it. I have a younger sister. I'll tell you the gory details another time, if you'll let me put it off. I decided on NYU. I considered Berkeley, mostly because it would get me to the other side of the continent. But I decided downtown Manhattan would be a far enough remove. I loved NYU, and I started to get some little freelance writing work while I was in college. I took my apartment right after graduation, so it must be a dozen years, now. No, fifteen, actually."

"Thanks, Oliver. I'd never push you to tell anything you're not ready to share. Could I call you Ollie? I think I like the sound of it," Will said.

"Call me whatever you like, as long as you call me. That's the important thing. Will, tell me about your marriage—if you want to."

Will took a minute to consider his reply. "I dated both boys and girls when I was in college. I didn't think much about it. I chose people on a case-by-case basis. When Jennifer came along and we fell in love, I assumed that was it—that my choice was made. If she had stayed with me, then I think I'd have remained happily straight. Or maybe I'm deceiving myself. But Jennifer didn't stay with me. And I've felt more and more like a gay man, through the years. Even though I haven't acted on it. Until now."

"Will, you're a remarkable man. I feel honored to know you. They have a bar at the Boathouse, don't they? Why don't we go and have a mulled cider or something?"

Will stopped, embraced me, and kissed me deeply. "I'd do anything with you, Ollie," he said. I started to cry, just a little. Or perhaps it was the wind. We did go to the Boathouse, to round out our autumn fantasy with warmth and spice. Was it just a fantasy? I couldn't be certain. It felt real.

When we got back to the apartment, both of us were ready for some serious lovemaking. We stripped off our cold-weather gear and fell back into my bed. Will took charge. I was happy to follow his lead, obediently. He seemed to know exactly what he wanted, and I offered him every inch of my body. I'd have happily done anything he desired that would bring him pleasure. "Ollie, may I . . .?"

"Anything," I said. "You don't need to ask." Will's hands were warm, and they seemed to be everywhere, as did his mouth. My eyes never left his face as Will arranged his torso above mine. I opened my legs, to offer up my body completely. Will gripped my thighs and presented his dick. "Yes," I said. "Yes, Will. I want you." And he was in. I was afraid I might levitate with the ecstasy I experienced when Will Granger inhabited me for the first time. Perhaps I did. Perhaps my memory of that event is clouded by everything that followed it. But I'm certain it was as at least as lovely as any event of my life.

Afterward, I lit a fire in the living room fireplace. We put on robes and warmed ourselves in front of it. "Jesus, Will," I said. "How dare you make me so happy! How can I give you up when you go back to your real life in a few hours?"

"Ollie, please don't say that. We'll figure out a way to join our lives. To be together. If it's what you want."

"With all my heart," I said.

"Well then, we'll do it. But, you know, we haven't eaten since breakfast. What's for dinner?" He was right, of course. We made a delivery choice and set the table. We ate. We were mostly quiet during dinner. Will hadn't even left yet, and I was already developing that dull little ache around the heart that signals longing for what I can't have. Our weekend time was used up. Used well, but used. Will dressed in the clothes he arrived in, as we had planned. And then he left.

I went about the business of straightening up and getting ready for bed as if on autopilot. I watched some CNN accompanied by a large cognac. I turned out the light and lay wide awake for a while. It was only midnight. I would survive, after all. I'd been through much worse. Hadn't I?

Chapter Four

My sister Louisa was five years younger than me. She was only ten when the folks died in a plane crash. It was harder on her even than it was on me, I think. I sort of got over it. I don't think she ever really did. We spent the rest of our childhood in Scarsdale with Aunt Cynthia and Uncle Charles. I hated it. So did Louie. But it was really only three years for me, before I could go off to college.

When Louisa phoned that morning in late October, I was pleased to hear from her, as always. "Ollie, I need your help," she said. "Can I come to stay with you? And bring Rufus?"

"Of course," I said. "Betina's here. I'll ask her to put clean sheets on the bed. Just consider the back room yours, for as long as you want it." I was glad I could help. Perhaps it would relieve some of my guilt—that I had been unable to help her out of the black hole that was her childhood. Louie had had a tough time in the last years. She was a gifted pianist, but she seemed unable to focus on it or on any studies. She never completed a degree. When she finally broke away from Scarsdale it was to move into a "crack den"—or so I imagined it—uptown somewhere.

Our communication was spotty, but Louie phoned me now and then, and I had seen her a few times in recent years. I knew she had an affair with a man who was maybe a thief, and—I never knew for sure—maybe a pimp, too. I knew she bore a child and named him Rufus because she was a big fan of Rufus Wainwright. Rufie was a beautiful child. He looked a little like Louisa and also like his African American father. I knew the relationship that produced Rufus went very badly indeed and that Louie had a restraining order against her ex. I also suspected that she was using—heroin, I assumed.

I had made some weak attempts at helping Louie in the past. Maybe. Or maybe I lacked the moral courage to figure a way to be of genuine value to her. But no matter how much I loved my baby sister, I felt helpless to aid her. And yet she turned to me that October day. I did some quick math and calculated that Rufus must be eight years old. The two of them arrived about an hour later. Louie looked tired and stressed. Rufus seemed *very* quiet. I greeted them both warmly. I led them to the back room. "Maybe there's enough space to add a little cot, for Rufus to sleep on," I said.

"Oh, don't worry about it. We're used to sleeping together. It'll be fine." Louisa looked me straight in the eye and said, "Thank you, darling. I was desperate."

I embraced her warmly and said, "Would you like something to eat or drink?"

"Nothing for me, thanks. I'd like to take a nap. But I'll bet Rufus could use something." He agreed, but without much enthusiasm.

"Okay, then. You two settle in, and then come to the kitchen, Rufie. I'll see what we can scare up for you." I left them alone and went to the kitchen. I was treating the situation as the new normal. I had no idea how long they would be living with me, but I assumed it would be for the foreseeable future. It would hardly cramp my style. It was a week and a half after my dreamy weekend with Will, and I had only seen him once since then. I couldn't have Will, and I didn't want anyone else. I suggested a standing Friday dinner date. Will agreed. That way I could at least see him occasionally and perhaps even have some alone time now and then. It wasn't much, but I preferred it to not seeing Will at all.

Rufus came to the kitchen. I sat him down and gave him a peanut butter sandwich (on good bread from Eli's) and some ginger ale. "Thanks, Uncle Ollie," he said.

"Enjoy it, little man," I said. "I don't know what you like, but we'll sort all that out. Maybe we can go food shopping tomorrow. Have you been to Zabar's?"

"I don't think so."

"You'll love it. They have everything—octopus, smoked eel, gefilte fish." Rufus grimaced. "I wanted to see if you were listening," I said. "They also have great peanut butter—as you now know—and chicken fingers. We won't starve. I have to do some work at my desk this afternoon. Do you want to watch a movie?"

"Sure," he said.

I led Rufus to the living room. "Let's keep the volume low so we don't disturb your mother. Let's see, how about *GONE WITH THE WIND*?" Rufus looked puzzled. "Maybe we'll save that for another day. You'll love it. All right, let me find something with no gun violence. That will be a challenge, but I think we can manage it." I found an animated Disney film that seemed reasonably harmless. I set it up, gave Rufus the remote, and retreated to my desk.

I phoned Will from my bedroom, to tell him my news. He asked what he could do to help.

"Besides loving me?" I asked.

"Besides loving you." he said.

"I have no idea, at the moment," I said. "But I'm sure I'll think of something. Why don't you and Sam come *here* on Friday, so you can meet my family? They'll love you, no doubt. How could they not?"

"Why don't I stop for Middle Eastern takeout on my way over, like I did for our weekend? Everyone likes that food, I think. Even kids. Sam always did."

"Bless you!" I said. "Will, I suspect you're a treasure," I said in my best Bette Davis voice. "Here then, on Friday, as early as you can. Thanks, Will, for everything."

"Please, Ollie, I'm at work. Don't make me get all mushy."

"Just get into my arms. Soon!" I said. I did some writing. I solved a tricky transition in a story, something that had eluded me. When I stepped into the living room to check on Rufus, I found him sound asleep. I figured he was exactly where he needed to be, so I lowered the volume even more and went back to my desk.

We got on with it. We went food shopping. We figured out a routine. Louisa was a much better cook than I am. She seemed to enjoy the humdrumness of it all. She seemed to be—okay, I guess. I never pressured her for information. She told me only what she felt I needed to know.

Louisa loved meeting Will that Friday night. Rufus also took to him. We had a warm, relaxed evening. Will was right: Rufus became a major hummus fan. After Will and Sam headed home, Louisa put Rufus to bed and came back to the kitchen to join me. I poured cognac. I didn't know if it was wise to give Louisa alcohol, but I also didn't think it was any of my business to make choices for her.

"Will's a wonderful man, Ollie," Louisa said. "I'm so happy for you."

"Thank you, darling," I said, "but it's complicated. He has Sam, as you know, and a life that has nothing to do with me. I don't know if we'll ever be able to— combine. I just don't know."

"Ollie, you have many talents," Louisa said, "but I always thought that what you do best is love. It's not always easy. You do it well. Don't stop now." I got a little weepy. We sat quietly for a bit. And then Louisa said, "Ollie, there's something I've never told you. I never wanted to burden you with it, but I think you need to know." And that was when Louisa filled me in on the deepest darkness of her childhood. I can't say I was shocked. Mostly I felt stupid for not having seen it.

The next morning, when Rufus and I were having breakfast, he said, "Mr. Granger seems like a nice guy."

"He is," I said. "Also, I love him very much. Are you okay with that?" Rufus flashed me his *Please, Uncle Ollie, don't treat me like a child* look. "Good," I said. "With everything that's going on in the world, a little more love is always a plus. Let's buy you a new pair of shoes. What do you say?" Rufus brightened noticeably. I suspected I'd end up paying for grossly overpriced sneakers in some hideous combination of colors.   But I knew that if they pleased Rufus, then they'd please me even more.

_______ *Chapter Five*

I got back to the apartment one afternoon in early November—after a meeting with a publisher about a writing project—to find Rufus pacing the living room floor like a caged animal. He ran to me and grabbed me. "Mom's not breathing," he said. "Do something!" I dashed to the back room and found Louie unresponsive, as Rufus had said. I grabbed her, shook her, slapped her, and called 911, all at the same time, or so it seemed. I even tried what I could remember of CPR chest compressions. Nothing worked. Paramedics arrived within a few minutes. They had no more success, despite state-of-the-art resuscitation gear.

I was numb. Rufus was hyper. He threw himself at the body as they took his mother away. I sprang into action and wrapped my arms around him. "Don't, Rufie," I said. "She's gone. We've lost her." I had no more words. I continued to hold him—to restrain him, really—as the EMS crew made their exit. I wasn't handling the situation any better than Rufus was. Just more quietly. If I had been in my apartment alone, trying to deal with the loss, I'd have probably retreated into a near-catatonic state. But that was not an option, with Louie's child in my arms.

"Rufie, take some deep breaths. We're going to get through this. We're going to get through this, God damn it!" I wasn't certain which of us I was trying to convince. "If I let go of you, do you think you could just sit quietly for a few minutes? Because if you're not ready, that's okay, too. I can hold you for days, if necessary. Maybe years. Who knows? I'm stronger than I look." I wondered how true that was.

"Okay, Uncle Ollie. You can let go of me. I won't do anything crazy."

"Good," I said. And I did release him. He was quiet, as promised. I extended my hand and said, "Come to the kitchen with me. I think we've both earned a drink." Rufus took my hand, and I led the way. I sat him down at the kitchen table and asked, "What'll it be, Buster? We have tomato juice; we have apple juice; we have milk; we have bourbon."

"Bourbon, please," Rufus said.

"Coming right up," I said as I poured him some apple juice—with a few ice cubes and a straw. I poured myself a large glass of wine. I joined him at the table. We sat, sipped, and stared into space for a while. Then I broke the silence. I said, "I meant it, Rufie. We'll get through this. I won't shit you: You know as well as I do it won't be easy. But we'll deal with it. Just hang on, little man. I've got you. We'll get through this together."

Rufus started to cry. So did I. We sat for a while. Eventually, I said, "Okay, we have to make some sense of the rest of today. Why don't you go take a nap?" Rufus eyed the direction of the back room with a look of terror. "In my room," I said. "Just take off your shoes and get under the covers for a little while. I have to make some phone calls." He looked skeptical, but he did as he was told.

I started making calls. I phoned Jerry first. I wanted him to know. Louie adored him, and he her. I just gave him the news and promised to call back the next day. Then I phoned my attorney. She's also a trusted friend. Priscilla is the toughest advocate I've ever known, and I suspected some tough advocacy might be needed. She promised to contact the Office of Children and Family Services and any other agency with an interest in the case.

I didn't quite remember—until the cold reality of Louie's death began to sink in—that I had Rufus's birth certificate in the little safe under my bed. Louisa had asked me to keep it for her. I told Prissy the name of the man who might be Rufie's father, and I told her he was not named on the certificate. Louie had been quite clear about that.

Priscilla offered to start the process of settling Louisa's estate. Was there a will? Who knew? I asked Prissy to do what she could, and I promised to hunt for any relevant documents. Mostly I wanted her to research Louie's trust fund and arrange to reassign it to her son—for his college and whatever else it might yield. And, of course, I told Priscilla what she might expect from Scarsdale. She said she would be armed and ready. I let go of some of my fears on the legal front.

Then I phoned Will. He took my call, fortunately. He validated my loss with perfect compassion. "I love you, Ollie," he said. "Call me whenever you want to. I know you and Rufus have a lot to deal with. I won't intrude, but I'm here, whenever you need me." I thanked him. Finally, I phoned Aunt Cynthia and Uncle Charles. I gritted my teeth as I anticipated their reaction to my news.

Louie hated them, entirely. She had valid reasons. I suppose I hated them as well. But my reasons were more about their inability to stand in adequately for the parents I had loved. Or at least I think I loved them. I'm not always certain these days. But I knew I didn't want Cynthia and Charles anywhere near Louie's body. I didn't want them involved in decisions that needed to be made. And—most emphatically—I did not want them involved with the future of her child. But they were blood, after all—Cynthia, anyway—and I couldn't ignore them.

"Really, Oliver, how could you let this happen under your roof?" Cynthia asked.

"Rufus and I are doing our best to get through this, Aunt Cynthia. I'm sure you didn't mean to be unkind. It's quite a shock for all of us, of course," I said. "I'll phone you tomorrow." I hung up as quickly as I could. You know I muttered things under my breath. You know I thought, *Vicious cunt!* And—the rest doesn't bear repeating.

That was all the phone work I was prepared to deal with that afternoon. Something told me to go and change the bed in the back room. Just as I returned to the kitchen, Rufus resurfaced from his nap. "Goodness, little man," I said. "I think you grew an inch taller while you were sleeping. Let that be a lesson to you, if you want to grow up strong and tall."

"Uncle Ollie, I think you're full of shit," Rufus said.

I sat him down at the kitchen table, replenished our beverages, and joined him. I looked him straight in the eye and said, "Rufie, you can hate me, if you want to. I can take it. You can be as angry as you want. You're entitled. Maybe I get it. My parents abandoned me, too. Your mother did her very best for you. And it wasn't good enough. Well, little man, fuck it! Life's not fair. But I'm here. And I'm going to take care of you. And I'm hoping you'll accept that. I'm hoping you'll let me love you enough to make up for everything you've lost. I do, you know. I love you, Rufus."

"Mother said she loved me. Uncle Charles and Aunt Cynthia say they love me."

"If you'd rather live with them, just tell me. I'll help you pack your things."

"Really?"

"Scarsdale is lovely. You'll be very happy there."

"I don't know," he said.

"Hey! Don't be an asshole! You're not going anywhere if I can help it. Rufie, we're blood. We belong together. You'll live here, and you'll start school in January, and you'll like it. You're a smart boy—as well as a smart-ass. You'll do well. And then you'll graduate, and you'll go to Harvard, or Columbia, or God-knows-where. And you'll get a job you love. And I'll dance at your wedding. What do you think, little man? Life could be worse."

"I think you're crazy, Uncle Ollie. But *good* crazy."

"Now that that's established," I said, "we need to make some dinner plans. Grief is hungry work. What do you think?" Rufus had no input, so I made an executive decision: I ordered pizza and salad from my local. We set the kitchen table and settled in to wait for the delivery. It was prompt. We ate. I poured myself another glass of wine. After supper I said, "Well, Rufus. It's just the two of us now. I loved your mother very much. She was mine before she was yours, even. I'll miss her every day, as long as I live. How do you feel, little man?"

"I don't know, Uncle Ollie."

"Of course you don't," I said. "That was a stupid question. You'll have to be patient with me. I've learned how to speak to adults—reasonably well. Kids? Not so much. We have to get to know each other. Rufie, you can tell me anything. You can ask me anything. I'm here. I'm not going anywhere— without you. I'm going to do my best to keep you safe. And that's all that matters for now. Why don't you get some sleep?" Rufus took my hand, and I led him to the back bedroom—his mother's room. And there was the bed where she died. A change of sheets wouldn't be enough to undo that horror. Maybe some day—even some day soon—he could learn to accept that reality. But I decided it didn't need to be that very night.

I said, "Look, Rufie, we can fix up this room. We can paint it whatever color you like, and you can stick all sorts of awful posters on the walls. You can do whatever you want with it. It's yours, Rufe. We can start tomorrow. Your old uncle is still pretty good with a paint roller." Rufus was on the verge of tears, as was I. I swept him up into my arms and held him as tenderly as if he were my own infant.

"I think we've both had enough excitement for one day," I said as I put him down. "Come with me." I led him to the living room, where I sat him down. "Okay, I think you can stay up a little later tonight. We could watch some TV. And when we're ready to turn in, Rufie, the chaise in my bedroom is very com- fortable. We'll put sheets on it. You can sleep there tonight and for as long as you want. Until you're ready."

"You have such a big bed, Uncle Ollie," he said. "Why can't I sleep with you?"

"You ask the tough questions, Rufie. That's a very good thing. And here's your answer: Little boys don't sleep in the same bed with adult men. Not in this culture, anyway. If the Child Protective Services thought you were sleeping in my bed, they would take you away immediately. And I couldn't bear to lose you. If anyone asks you where you're sleeping, you can say 'on the sofa, until my room is ready.' And that will be the truth. We have to play by the rules. Well, those rules, anyway. We'll talk later about the ones we want to break."

"Uncle Ollie, do you really want me here?"

"More than I can tell you, little man. I've never had a child. Never wanted one. Until you came along. But—I don't know if I should say this or not—I want to be the best father I can be to you. If you'll have me."

"I don't know much about my father. I only saw him, like, twice. And he made Mom cry. I don't know what to think of him."

"You don't have to decide that tonight. Take all the time you need. I'm going to do everything for you that your father would do if he were here to take care of you. Look, I don't know about you, little man, but it's way past my bedtime. Could we talk about this in the morning?"

"Sure," he said. "I know old people need their rest."

"And you'd better know that a smart-ass gets what's coming to him," I said as I chased him to my bedroom. We laughed and roughhoused like kids. He *was* one, after all. And he brought out the kid in me, I think. We made up the chaise for Rufus. I tucked him in. I didn't sing him a lullaby. I didn't know how. Perhaps I would have to learn. Instead, I said, "Sleep well, precious boy." I kissed him on the forehead, and then I went to my bed and turned out the light.

I lay there for a while with my eyes wide open. I thought, *Can I do this? Can I take care of Louie's child? Can I even get permanent custody of him? And, if not, could I give him up? Could my heart stand to lose his mother and Rufus both?* I had no answers, of course. Eventually, I grew weary of worry, and I slept.

Chapter Six

Sometime after 2:00, Rufus began to wheeze. Loudly. It was a bark, really. I was horrified, of course. I jumped out of bed, threw on my robe, and grabbed him. I ran to my bathroom and bounced Rufus on my hip as I turned on the shower with straight hot water and closed the bathroom door. I sat on the toilet with Rufus on my lap. I had a vague memory from childhood of a late-night bout with croup—whatever the fuck that is.

I didn't know whether Rufus was having a bad dream or a respiratory attack. But I took action. I sat with him while the steam enveloped us. I held him. "Just breathe," I said. "I've got you. There is absolutely nothing bad that can happen to you tonight. I'm here. You're safe." Did I rock him in my arms? Did I bounce him on my knees? Did I hum— softly—his favorite Beatles song? All of the above, surely.

It was a gradual thing, as we sat there in the thickening steam. But Rufus's breathing began to normalize. When I sensed that he was stable, I simply turned off the water and sat back down with him on my lap for another ten minutes or so. I didn't ask Rufus how he felt. I didn't say anything. We both needed sleep rather than verbal stimulation. When I was certain that Rufus was ready to go back to bed, I carried him to the chaise and tucked him in, again. He was asleep almost before his head hit the pillow. I had a similar experience. But, in my case, before I dropped off, I sent a fervent prayer to the Universe requesting that I might be spared a repeat of our last little drama. And yet, I knew that anything is possible.

I'm just an okay cook, but I do like breakfast. I thought we both deserved something substantial. So in the morning I toasted some good bread, threw some Canadian bacon slices into a skillet, and soft-boiled some eggs. I served Rufus a breakfast coffee that was 99% hot milk. He said he liked it. And so I said, "I guess there's hope for you after all."

"Who's the child at this table?" he asked.

"Jesus, Rufe!" I said. "You sure are a New York City kid."

"Oooh, this egg is gooey," he said.

"Shut up and eat it," I said. "These are free-range organic eggs that cost six times what supermarket eggs cost. Dip the toast into the goo. You'll like it." Rufus was tentative, but he gave it a try. I could tell by the look on his face that he *did* like it. I was relieved. The last thing I wanted to deal with was a picky eater. He ate.

"Is that bedroom really mine?" he asked.

"You bet. What color paint did you have in mind? I was thinking chartreuse."

"Is that sort of green?" he asked.

"Smart boy! I always said that, didn't I? I think you take after me. You *look* like me, actually. Did you ever notice that?" Rufus rolled his eyes. He also ate his breakfast and thanked me for it. "You don't have to thank me for anything," I said. "But I'm glad you want to, because it shows you have a good heart.

"I know I said we could start on your room this morning, but I was thinking maybe we could go to the park instead. There won't be that many more fall days like this before the serious cold sets in. There's a fountain near the center of the park that you should see. It's most beautiful in late spring, but I love it in all seasons. You need to meet the angel. All New Yorkers should. And then we could walk to the Met Museum and have a snack in one of the cafés. We can't play hooky every day, but I think we've both earned some down time. What do you think?"

"I think, yes," Rufus said.

"Smart man," I said. "Okay, then. Have a quick shower. And don't forget to brush your teeth. And change your underwear. Jesus! I'm turning into my mother. Nevertheless, don't forget to brush your teeth. And change your underwear. I'll meet you at the front door in thirty minutes. And wear something warm." I felt buoyant. I felt a new kind of happiness. I felt *needed*. I felt human.

Aunt Cynthia scheduled a funeral at Campbell's. I gave in on that one point in exchange for simple cremation. Subjecting Louie's body to embalming and interment in family soil would have been too horrible. We compromised. I had to find something somber for Rufus to wear. Luckily, Will brought us a dark suit Sam had outgrown. It fit Rufus fine. The two of us dressed that morning, and I said, "Rufie, when did you become so handsome? You do your mother proud." And then I grabbed him and wrapped my arms around him. I said, "Rufe, you don't have to do this if you don't want to. Aunt Cynthia can take care of it all by herself."

I had my own early memories of funerary horrors. I'd have spared Rufus the pain if I could have done it. But it doesn't really work that way, of course. He, said, "I'm good, Uncle Ollie." We waited for the call on the house phone telling us the car was waiting. I gave Rufus one last chance to back out. He kept a stiff upper lip. We headed downstairs and got into a big black car for the trip across town.

Only a few dozen people attended: some family; a few friends of Louie's; Jerry, of course; Priscilla. Will came, which I thought very sweet of him. It was—a funeral. I couldn't help thinking how much Louie would have hated it. But it seemed that Rufus and I had little more choice than *she* did in the matter. At least it wasn't graveside. At least we didn't have to listen to, "In sure and certain hope of the resurrection . . . earth to earth, ashes to ashes, dust to dust." That would have sent me howling. Instead, we listened to polite memorial speak. And then it was over.

Most of the attendees came to my apartment after the service—for stiff drinks and a bite to eat. Betina had offered to organize things, and I was delighted to let her do it. Soon after we all arrived, Aunt Cynthia came to me and asked if we could speak privately. I looked around. Rufus was safely under Will's wing. Betina was feeding people and making sure they got drinks. I figured I could disappear for a few minutes without mishap. I led Cynthia to my bedroom and closed the door behind us.

"Charles and I want to make sure that everything is being done properly for the child," she said."

"I can assure you that everything *is* being done properly for Rufus," I said.

"Where is he sleeping?" she asked.

"On the sofa, until his room is ready," I said. I knew the drill as well as Rufus did.

"We think he should live with us," Cynthia said.

I took a deep breath. "I don't want to be nasty, and I don't mean to be mean. But I hope I only have to say this once. When Louisa needed help, she came to me. And she brought her child. She did *not* go to you, nor would she ever have done so, under any circumstance. She came to *me*. And she left her child with *me*. This is a terrible situation for all of us, but please, I beg you, *stay out of it!* If you want to be involved, then set up a college fund for Rufus. He's a smart boy. I told him Harvard is his best bet. We'll see. But please, just let us get on with it."

"Charles and I don't feel it's appropriate for the child to be living here with you," Cynthia said. That was all the encouragement I needed to take off the gloves.

"Speaking of appropriate, I think a judge would be very interested to hear what Louisa told me about her childhood with you two," I said.

"There was nothing to tell, I'm sure," she said.

"In that case, you won't mind if I tell the judge— are you sure you want to go there?" I asked her.

"Oliver, you can say whatever you please. My conscience is clear."

"I think it's important for the judge to know that Louisa told me Uncle Charles molested her regularly from ages ten to fifteen, at which point she learned how to fight him off. And that you did nothing to protect her. I'm sure that's the main reason she hated both of you so intensely. But I suspect there were other reasons as well."

"That's a foolish lie, Oliver. No one will believe it," Cynthia said.

"That's up to the judge, isn't it?" I asked. "Please think about it. I have no qualms about airing the truth in public. If you push this, then it will be my duty—as well as a great pleasure—to tell my truth. But if you back off, then it can remain our dirty secret. Your choice."

I had taken a bit of the wind out of Aunt Cynthia's sails. She was never meek, but she came down from her high dudgeon enough to say, "I'll speak to Charles about it."

"Good," I said. "And you might tell him that if *I* have to discuss the matter with him, then it will be time to consider criminal charges. And, by the way, you met Priscilla Lawson. She knows a great deal about me and Louisa and Rufus, and also about you and Uncle Charles. She *doesn't* know about this. If I tell her, then it might be entirely out of my hands. She's a principled advocate. She has a responsibility to the law, as well as to her client. I'm hoping we can settle this matter, you and I, quickly. In fact, I'm hoping that you'll phone me tomorrow morning to tell me that you two are stepping aside from any interference in the custody petition that will go before the Family Court soon. Aunt Cynthia, we've rarely underestimated each other in the past, I think. Dismiss me now at your peril. I will not be moved in this."

Our parting was icy, of course. But I felt I had taken not just the first set but perhaps the match. When I got back to the living room—buzzing with righteous anger—Rufus was still talking to Will. I was relieved. It was difficult for me to look Uncle Charles in the eye, as it had been for years. At one point I suspected he was heading toward Rufus, and I managed to block his access. At least I could offer Rufus the protection his mother had been denied.

Eventually, the guests went home. Scarsdale left early, to my great relief. Prissy had an appointment. Jerry, too. Family and friends said their goodbyes and condolences and peeled off. And then it was just Will, Betina, Rufus, and me. A sense of safety returned to my home. Betina straightened up the party things. I thanked her. I paid her twice what she had requested. *She* thanked *me.* She left. "Rufie, why don't you go and change?" I said. He was happy to do so, of course.

"Will," I said, "what a blessing it's been to have you with me today. I wish it could have been a happier occasion. We have so little time together."

"Tell me," Will said. "I'm going to leave. I know you and Rufus need to be alone. Oliver, I love you," he said, and he kissed me warmly. And he was gone. Great waves of loss flowed over me. And then Rufus returned from his room dressed in his pajamas. I reached for him. He let me pick him up and hold him. He even embraced me in return.

"Well, little man," I said, "that was quite a day. Let's not do that again any time soon."

"That's creepy, Uncle Ollie," he said.

"Quite right. But you were perfect today. I was so proud of you, Rufie. You got through all that family shit, and all that funeral shit. Everything else is going to be easy. You believe that, don't you? Let's have a drink." We went to the kitchen table. I had bought some pomegranate juice the day before. I laced Rufie's apple juice with it. He said he liked it, so I tried a splash in my wine. I liked it, too.

We sat for a while and sipped our beverages. I'm not certain which of us started to weep first. Rufus began to choke on his tears. I said, "Don't fight it, Rufie. That will only make you sick. Let it out. I told you we're going to get through this. We're going to feel it, and some day we're going to accept it and move on. But that won't happen one breath sooner than when we're ready. I'm going to try to be very gentle with you during the process, and I hope you'll be gentle with me as well. I don't have all the answers. But I'm doing my best. We'd better get you some supper," I said.

I put together a little meal for Rufus from the party fare. It contained *most* of the important food groups. I joined him. Afterward I said, "I think we've earned a movie. How about *THE WIZARD OF OZ?*"

"That's the one with the witches?" he asked. "Like Aunt Cynthia?"

"Watch your mouth, kid," I said. "You're not old enough to make cracks like that. I'll tell you when you have permission. Meanwhile, you'll keep a civil tongue in your head while you're under my roof." Rufus rolled his eyes. He also got the message, I hoped, that he had a responsibility to behave carefully until we were entirely out of the legal woods.

"Yes, the one with the witches. Go brush your teeth, and I'll set it up."

"Can we watch in the bedroom? Can I sit on your bed to watch?'

"Just this once," I said. "But if you tell anyone you've been on my bed, I swear I'll put you in an or- phanage." I regretted that instantly, of course. I grabbed him and said, "Rufie, please forgive me for trying to make a really bad joke. You know you're not going anywhere, no matter what, don't you?"

"Sure, Uncle Ollie," he said.

"I asked you to be gentle with me. Maybe you didn't know how hard that can be sometimes, with people we love. I'm going to try my best not to be stupid. Go brush your teeth." He did. I took off my suit and hung it up. I slipped out of the rest of my funeral drag and put on a robe. When Rufus came to my room, I invited him up onto my bed and asked him, "So what do you think, little man? Can you forgive me for being an asshole?"

"Of course, Uncle Ollie," he said. "I can tell when you're serious and when you're just being an . . . "

"That's enough of that," I said. "You've been through a lot, Rufe, and you've earned a lot. But you're not *there* yet. You can't speak to me or anyone else that way. For now. We'll both know when that time comes. Meanwhile, Dorothy is waiting for you." I started the picture. It remains magical after all these years and after over-zealous restorations, I think. Rufus was enchanted. And so was I.

Chapter Seven

Scarsdale did back out of the legal picture. I was relieved, to say the least. When Aunt Cynthia phoned me, she said their attorney would set up a trust fund for Rufus. That was welcome news, but it wasn't a done deal. I assumed there was plenty of money there. Mother and Cynthia had shared their parents' estate. Charles had family money, too, plus a successful business in town. They had no children. The money had to go somewhere. I would have been delighted if they decided to settle the whole thing on Rufus. I would also have been pleased if they decided on half to Rufus and half to me. I'm not stupid. I would have taken their money in a heartbeat.

But whatever they decided, it would all take a while, of course. Priscilla assured me we had a good case for permanent custody. And there was no interference from Child Protective Services. So perhaps Rufus could actually stay with me and live a reasonably normal life. I took nothing for granted, but I tried to get on with *my* life, such as it was. I had work to do. That was a great distraction. I was finishing up the celebrity "autobiography" and starting on a new project—a book about whales. I hoped that one would please Rufus. In fact, pleasing Rufus and doing the right things for him were my main focus.

In the quiet days after the funeral, I had to figure out a routine for both of us. But first I had to get Rufus enrolled in school. I found one nearby with a good reputation. I never thought much about it when I was growing up, but I knew that the right school can make all the difference in a child's future. I hadn't a clue where there might be some school records. I told the admissions lady that Rufus had been home schooled, and that his mother had just died. Hence, the need for a new situation. It was largely the truth.

It was starting to look iffy, but I suggested they test his intelligence and his grade level. The admissions lady agreed. I hated to put Rufus through the process, but I made light of it and told him to just go in and smile a lot: "You have a great smile, Rufus," I said. "Use it. Just take whatever stupid tests they give you and everything will be fine." And it was fine. Rufus was accepted! The fact that the school was looking to increase diversity in the student body probably did him no harm. But he was in, for whatever reasons.

I'd have preferred to keep Scarsdale out of it entirely, but the fees were so high that I couldn't have managed it alone. When I told Aunt Cynthia we were talking maybe $45K a year, she didn't even gulp before saying, "I'll speak to Charles about it." I assumed that Cynthia and Charles would pick up the school bills. I proceeded accordingly. Rufus wouldn't start school until January. Meanwhile, I wanted to keep his brain active. I found books for him to read—things on a reading list from his school that he could download to my tablet, plus books I owned that I hoped he would read and love. He was too young for Jane Austen, I reasoned, but maybe Jack London instead.

I also wanted to keep Rufie's body active, so I enrolled him in a swimming class at my gym. We picked out trunks, a swim cap, and goggles at a sporting goods shop. I began to match my gym schedule to Rufie's class schedule, so we could arrive, work out, and then head home together. I wasn't ready for him to go out on his own, even though I lived in a safe neighborhood. Surely I would get over that soon enough, but I wasn't ready to let go of him. Not yet.

Rufus decided on red for his room. We painted it, together, with black trim on the moldings and door frames. It looked pretty good, actually. Not so good that I was ready to give *my* room the same color scheme, but good. We found bed sheets with the same colors. It all came together. In time, with lots of living, it would become a wonderful room. But even newly minted, it showed great promise.

Days were long. I missed Will terribly. We kept our Friday dinner dates. Sometimes I cooked for him, and sometimes he brought Sam with him. Sam was two years older than Rufus, so I doubted they would strike up much of a friendship. But to my pleasant surprise, they did seem to bond. That was a plus. Will seemed pleased, too. On the Fridays Will cooked for us, I always took Rufus with me. He would disappear into Sam's room, giving Will and me a few minutes of almost-alone time.

There would also be some Fridays when Will and I wanted to go to the theatre or a concert or just have dinner alone. Sometimes Betina was available to stay with Rufus, and sometimes Jerry volunteered.

He made Rufus laugh, so he was always the favorite babysitter. One Friday night, after I got back to the apartment, Rufus came out of his room to greet me. I gave him a big hug and sent him back to bed. Jerry said, "Do you know what that little scamp asked me? Rufus wanted to know if you have a big dick."

"Shit!" I said. "What did you say?"

"I said, 'What kind of question is that, little creep? Why do you want to know?' "

"And?"

"He said, 'I just want him to be popular. I don't think he has enough friends.' I assured Rufus you have all the popularity any man needs, and that he might better focus on his *own* popularity."

"Jerry, please don't encourage him," I said. "We have to maintain some semblance of propriety if we're going to make this living arrangement permanent. So, you really think I'm popular?"

"I always did. But you know that," Jerry said. "It's been a while, but I'd be happy to prove it. Even though we're best friends, now, I could wrap my lips around your popularity like I did when we were lovers. Do you remember?"

"Do I remember?" I asked. "Jerry, those were such sweet days. Maybe we were too young to appreciate them. I don't know. I'm not even certain what went wrong with us. I always thought it was because you had a crush on that guy, Gabriel. He was one hot number, I'll give him that. But I've never been certain why we lost . . . what we had."

"I have a bit of that amnesia, too," Jerry said. "I remember Gabriel, believe me, even though he tried his best to fuck my brains out. I loved you so much, Ollie. Still do. I'm not sure I know any more than you do about why we called it off. Perhaps I've never told you this, but I've often wondered if we could try it again. I was just about to suggest it when you met Carlos. And believe me, that looked like forever to *me*, too. Now? I don't know."

"Jerry, you've been my lifeline for a lot of years. I just said good night to a man I've been wanting to wrap my life around. And I won't see him again until next Friday, most likely. It doesn't matter how many times we speak on the phone during the week. It's not the same as holding him. I can't see where it's going, but then the most important thing in my life is Rufus's future. Everything else seems trivial in comparison. Please don't talk to me about might-have-beens or maybe-tomorrows. I don't have time for that now."

"You're absolutely right, Ollie," Jerry said. "That blow job will have to wait. But the offer stands."

"I love you, Jerry," I said. "You know that, don't you?"

"It's what I live for," he said. "Get some rest, my dear. Phone me tomorrow. And don't forget to pay me for my babysitting services tonight. I would accept dinner. Maybe with the Munchkin. He's priceless." Jerry kissed me, very sweetly. It conjured up many memories. Jerry's kiss felt comfortable. It felt right. It also felt confusing. Surely Will's was the only kiss I craved. Wasn't it?

📖

Will wanted to cook Thanksgiving dinner. I insisted we all go out to a restaurant in the neighborhood. Nora, too. It was adequate food. I was full of gratitude. After our meal, Nora headed home with the boys, and Will came to my apartment for the evening. It was our first time alone together in a month and a half. I prefer not to make love on an overstuffed stomach, but necessity has a way of changing the rules.

Will in my bed again made me feel my heart might burst. Or was it too much turkey? We held each other as tenderly as if it were our last time together, as indeed it might be. I assumed nothing, not even Will's love for me. I was grateful to have him in my arms. It would have to be enough. We were both too full for anything acrobatic. Instead we quietly enjoyed each other and pulled off a mutual orgasm that was as satisfying for me as anything we had shared. There was cum everywhere, or so it seemed. I blended it, and we both savored the mix. There's always room for that dessert.

I hated knowing our evening together would end. But I got on with it. We cleaned up a little, dressed, and headed out together. The wind had picked up, and there was a nasty bite to it. We rewrapped our scarves and walked to Will's apartment arm in arm. As we reached the lobby of his building, I instinctively went into straight-man mode. I didn't like it, but I knew how to play the game.

When we got to Will's apartment, I realized that Rufus hadn't missed me even slightly. He and Sam were busy with a video game. I dragged Rufus away from the game and bundled him up for our walk. We said our goodbyes and thank-yous and headed home. "Did you and Mr. Granger have a good time?" he asked me on our way.

"Yes, we always have a good time when we're together."

"That isn't very often. Why is that?" Rufus asked.

"My, aren't you full of questions tonight! But I told you to ask me anything, didn't I? Well, here's my best answer: Mr. Granger and I have separate lives. He has Sam, and his work, and his apartment. I have you, and *my* work, and *my* apartment. Our lives don't really blend very well. You'll learn that loving someone is not always enough. But it's a good start. And those are my last words on the subject of love for tonight. I hope you were listening," I said.

"I always listen when you talk to me," Rufus said.

"Yeah, sure, and do you have a bridge for sale?" I asked.

"Huh?"

"Never mind, little man. That joke is older than time, and you'll never need to know it. Are you warm enough? 'Cause I could carry you the rest of the way, inside my coat."

"I'm good, Uncle Ollie," Rufus said.

"I think we need to buy you some winter clothes. Why don't we go shopping tomorrow, after the gym?"

"Sure, Uncle Ollie. Whatever you say."

As we crossed Columbus Avenue I said, "I say, I'm going to race you home. I'm expecting a fair fight. If you let me win, then I'll starve you till Christmas." Rufus took off like a shot. I decided I might have a budding track star on my hands. I couldn't keep up with him, so he reached the front door of our building as I was rounding the corner. We were both laughing and out of breath. Enough time had passed since our feast that we were in no danger of losing it. Rufus and I headed to the apartment and got ready for bed. It was a day well spent.

December used to be my favorite month. When I was a child, the first snow of a Westchester winter made me tingle. Mother always decorated the house for Christmas, and the sights and sounds and smells of the holiday season brought me much excitement. It all changed after the folks died, of course. And, as always, Louisa got the worst of it. She was only ten when we were wrenched out of our home and plopped down in some other house, in Scarsdale. Christmas was never the same again.

All those memories were fresh in my mind as I contemplated celebrating yet another Christmas—but this time minus Louisa and plus her child. I wanted Rufus to have a good experience. I was conflicted about how much Christianity I wanted to foist on him. I had loved the whole Christ Child thing at his age. I wasn't so sure about it for the present day. "What did your mother tell you about Christmas?" I asked Rufus.

"She said, 'Jesus was a good guy, but Christmas is mostly about big churches and big business.' "

"Sounds right to me," I said. "So how do you want to celebrate this year, little man?"

"I don't care, Uncle Ollie, as long as we can be together. Let's do whatever *you* want to do."

I was floored. Rufus had never actually said he wanted to be with me. I hoped he did. I had made plans in that direction. I even had legal action pending. And a fresh coat of paint in the back room. But there was Rufus's first affirmation of the future I envisioned. So, it wasn't just my fantasy after all. He really wanted me to parent him. I was speechless for a bit. Eventually I said, "We'll think of something fun. Have you been naughty or nice?"

"Don't give me that Santa Claus shit," Rufus said.

"Hey! Your mouth!" I said. "You know better than to talk that way to me. Or to any adult. Or am I delusional?"

"Sorry, Uncle Ollie. You're right. But what about Mr. Granger? Don't you want to spend Christmas with him?"

"Very much," I said, "but only if that includes you. We'll come up with something. Don't worry about it." And that's what we did.

Chapter Eight

As much as I had lost most of my interest in holidays, I still wanted Rufie to enjoy himself. We went ice-skating at the Wollman Rink in Central Park. We went to Serendipity for overrated desserts. It's such a charming place, I never mind that the food is underwhelming. We went to Bloomingdale's. I asked Rufus to choose a gift for himself—something he always wanted but wouldn't dare to ask for. Within reason, of course.

He couldn't do it. He said he couldn't think of anything he wanted that he didn't already have. "We'll fix that," I said. I grabbed his hand and we dashed to the men's department. Sure enough, they had a cashmere scarf in a lovely shade of chartreuse. "This is you, Rufie," I said. "It makes your eyes look golden. You should always wear this color."

He flashed me his *You're full of shit, Uncle Ollie* look. But he also touched the scarf. And who can fail to respond to the luxury of that texture? Rufus let me drape the scarf around him and show him how he looked in a mirror. "What do you think, little man?" I asked. "Could you accept this as a gift? If it isn't good enough, we'll find something else. But I'm pretty smart about things sartorial, and I say yes."

"Yes, Uncle Ollie," Rufus said. "I love it. But, sartorial? What's that?"

"Oh, Rufus. You have to start a list. Are you keeping a journal? Maybe we need to take you to stationery and get you a Moleskine." I never thought I'd become Auntie Mame, and yet there I was poised to transform a boy's life and maybe teach myself how to live at the same time. Christmas was coming, and the only gift Rufus really needed was his mother's return—but that was the one gift beyond any powers I knew. And yet, it was up to me to make the best of it.

I nearly stopped worrying about whether or not I could do it. Nearly. I spoke to Will that evening. He suggested the Christmas Eve midnight mass at St. John the Divine. I thought that was a wonderful idea. It's such a beautiful church, and I hoped Rufus might be just a bit awed by it. And staying up so far past his bedtime would surely be a treat. Yes.

We survived the holidays. I'd have preferred more Will, but we did get to see each other a bit more than usual. We weren't alone, but at least we were together—for Christmas Eve, dinner on Christmas Day, and then New Year's Eve. I thought I might have to carry Rufus home from Will's after we ushered in the New Year. But he stayed wide awake until we made it home. It was all I could do to get teeth brushed—Rufus's and mine—before we both conked out.

I was looking forward to the quietness of January, but I was also dreading "the talk" I assumed I had to give Rufus before sending him out into the world. What the hell did I know about what he needed to know? At breakfast on New Year's Day, I asked him, "What did your Mom tell you about being black?" I figured I might as well get right to the point.

"She told me people are afraid of anyone different. She told me I have to stay away from any situation that can go wrong, because some people will always assume it's my fault. She told me to be polite at all times, especially with policemen. She said some cops are looking for any excuse to interact with a black kid, so I shouldn't give them one."

"I guess she covered the bases," I said. I should have known Rufus was way ahead of me on that subject. I just prayed he never had to use his mother's advice. Though surely he would. There was a cold snap, and the city was blanketed in white when I walked Rufus to his first day of school. He seemed unimpressed with the whole thing. I forgot sometimes how much he had already experienced in his young life. The first day of school didn't carry the same excitement it might for other children. Rufus took it in his stride. When I collected him at 3:00, he seemed unmoved by the day's events.

"So, what do you think, little man?" I asked. "Does the school meet your standards?"

"It's fine, Uncle Ollie. I like my teacher. She's pretty. Actually, she looks a little bit like Mom."

"What about the other students?" I asked.

"They all know each other, so they mostly ignored me. That's fine."

"Do you have any idea how proud I am of you, Rufus? Because I am. Every day." I *was* proud of him. I was also a little concerned about his friend-making skills. "When you're ready, you'll open up,"

I said. "You can have all the friends you want, Rufus. It's up to you. No pressure." Rufus flashed me his *You're full of shit, Uncle Ollie* look. "You're a charming guy," I said.

"Do you really think I'm charming, Uncle Ollie?"

"Well, you charmed the socks off me. And I'm a tough customer. You have all the charm you need, Rufus. And when you're ready to use it, there'll be no stopping you." He seemed at ease with the new situation. And that was the important thing, after all. I decided I could stop worrying about the school choice I had made. One less worry on my list.

One particularly cold day when I didn't feel much like cooking, I took Jerry and Rufus out to dinner at a neighborhood Italian place. I convinced Rufus to order the *primavera*-type pasta dish. I was always trying to get vegetables into him. He was a good sport. He was a terrific kid, actually. I don't know how I'd have dealt with special needs. Fortunately, I didn't have to.

"You two seem to be braving the cold," Jerry said. "Just be sure your balls don't freeze, Rufus. That can be really ugly." Rufus laughed. I was less mirthful.

"Jerry, please," I said. "Try to act like an adult." He didn't, of course. But Jerry's sense of play was a major part of why I had loved him so much for so many years. And I certainly didn't expect him to change. "Carry on, dear."

"Yes, dear. Rufus, did I ever tell you the one about the young man from Nantucket?"

"Let's save that for another cold winter's night, say, ten years from now," I suggested.

"Sorry, Rufe. Your mean old uncle says no limericks. Not to worry. I'll think of something else."

"No doubt you will," I said. "They gave me too much prosciutto. Who wants some of it?" Of course I was glad to see Rufus laugh. I worried that we didn't have enough laughter in our home. God knows Rufus deserved all the lightness he could get. I had been largely starved of humor in my childhood, I think. I didn't want that to happen to him. "What do you think, Rufus?" I asked. "Do you think we could grant Jerry honorary uncleship? *Honorary*, mind you. No votes or vetoes. If he wants it."

"With all my heart," Jerry said, with a very courtly gesture.

"Yes, please." Rufus said. "I always wanted an Uncle Jerry."

"See, Jerry? He takes after you already," I said. And then I improvised a small investiture ceremony, using a breadstick instead of a sword. The deed was done. And I began to feel I had made a good choice for Rufus's future. *Someone* had to head up the bullshit department. And of course, Jerry was the perfect choice.

Chapter Nine

The celebrity "autobiography" was getting great advance press. The book on whales was put on hold, but that's nothing unusual in publishing. It gave me time to find more work. I was underwhelmed by my career progress. But I was more concerned about running my household. It ran. Aunt Cynthia and Uncle Charles came through with the school expenses, as I had hoped, and they also offered a monthly payment toward Rufus's maintenance. Isn't guilt a wonderful thing! I took it, of course. It allowed me to focus even more on Rufus.

I walked him to school each morning, and then I picked him up at 3:00. We went to the gym on Mondays, Wednesdays, and Fridays. I always made sure there was a healthy snack available in the fridge when we got home. We had dinner, usually something I cooked. Rufus began to join in the preparation, a little. Sharp knives and open flames are a bit scary. I was careful to gauge his readiness for various tasks.

Occasionally, we had an evening out at a restaurant or at Jerry's. He's a better cook than I am, by far. On weekends we slept late, had a big breakfast, and went out in the afternoon to a movie or a museum. Natural History has an IMAX theater, so sometimes it was a movie *and* a museum. I had my

Friday nights with Will. They were always fun, but I began to wonder how I really felt about him. The lack of a real union began to take its toll on my emotions, I think. One Friday evening at dinner I asked him, "Will, how do you feel about our relationship? We don't really talk about it anymore. We get together on Fridays. I'm always thrilled to see you. But then . . .?"

"Ollie, I know exactly what you're asking," Will said. "I can't tell you how many times I've found myself daydreaming about you and your smile and your kiss and your voice and your butt and your dick and every other part of you. And I can't tell you how often I lie awake at night craving your presence—beside me, in my bed. *Aching* for you. But I can't figure out how to make it happen. I don't think you and Rufus want to move in with Sam and me. Although you're welcome. And I don't see Sam and me moving in with you and Rufus. I don't entirely understand why it has to be so complicated—for two people who love each other. You let me ramble on."

"Thanks, Will, for going there," I said. "I've been avoiding that territory, I think. I don't know how to solve that impasse, either. Perhaps I've been hoping that the Housing Fairy will wave the wand and join our households. Short of that? I don't see a solution either." We sat quietly for a bit. "Will, could we keep our Friday friendship? At least for a while? I can't have you, but I couldn't bear to lose you."

"Yes, Ollie," he said. "I'll keep our Fridays on my calendar, just as I keep you in my heart. Ollie, please don't rush into any changes. Please let our love have every chance to grow. Please don't give up on us. I haven't."

"I won't, Will. I promise." As I walked home that night, I started to shiver. My coat was warm enough. My scarf was tied properly. I was wearing gloves. And yet I found myself chilled to the bone. I set my jaw so my teeth wouldn't chatter. I broke into a sprint, for the last block home. Once upstairs, I thanked Betina for staying with Rufus. I paid her and sent her home. I looked in on him and kissed him on the forehead. He was so precious—waking or sleeping. I went to my room.

I was still shivering as I stripped and dashed to my bathroom. I started the shower and got myself under the hottest spray I could stand. It took a while for me to thaw. It took a lot of hot water, and it also took some tears. More than tears. Sobs. Several big ones. I felt so empty. And yet, of course, there was really nothing new, except that I had considered the full impossibility of my relationship with Will for maybe the first time. And it made me feel like shit.

I was grateful to Priscilla for her diligent work on the custody case. When the judge ruled in our favor—but provisionally, with another look at the situation in six months—I decided we should celebrate. I called her and invited her to dinner one evening the following week. "Should I bring Babby?" she asked.

"That goes without saying," I answered. I considered inviting Will and Sam. But then it occurred to me that maybe I had become too dependent on their friendship. Or something. I'm not certain exactly what I was feeling. It would have been lovely to have them with us. But I didn't invite them. We had two women who were lovers coming to our home. I assumed Rufus would be fine with that. But just to be certain, I ran it by him. "Did your mother tell you about lesbians?" I asked him.

"Is that two women, together?" he asked.

"Yes."

"She told me some people love the same sex, and others love the opposite sex. And that's just how we're made." I wished I were as smart as my little sister was. It would have made the parenting thing a whole lot easier. But every time something important came along, I discovered that Louie had already done the heavy lifting. And I was grateful.

"Your Uncle Jerry's coming, too," I said. Rufus brightened noticeably. "Do you want to invite someone from school? Six is the perfect number for a dinner party." Rufus was uncertain, so we left it open for a few days.

One afternoon, when I picked him up from school, Rufus said, "I invited a guy to dinner next week, and he said yes. He's new at school, too. So he doesn't know many people."

"Perfect," I said. It made me proud that "my child" thought to include a new kid who was swimming in the same unfamiliar waters he was. Rufus *was* a good kid. Definitely. I decided to prepare a beef stew, the day before the party, because it always seemed to turn out well and because it always tasted better the second day. Rufus helped me shop for the ingredients for the stew and for the rest of our meal. I looked at flowers for the table. I said, "Can you believe it, Rufie? It's February, and somebody is growing beautiful flowers." Rufus seemed less impressed than I was, but he helped with the selection. And then we headed home with all our goodies.

The afternoon of the party, Rufus helped me set the table. He also promised to make his bed and neaten his room. I didn't even have to ask. Smart kid. I wasn't in much of a panic about entertaining. I didn't do it very often, but I sort of knew how. It would be fine. I wanted everyone to have a good time, including me. We got dressed. I arranged the flowers in two low bowls for the dining table. They looked great. I lit some candles. I adjusted the lights. I called down to ask the doorman to send our guests right up. We were ready.

Jerry arrived first, right at 7:00, followed by the girls, a moment later. I embraced everyone. Priscilla said, "Ollie, the apartment looks great. And it smells wonderful in here." She handed me a very pretty bouquet of lavender roses. I had the perfect vase for them, luckily, and so I was able to quickly get them on a table in the living room. They looked terrific. Jerry poured wine.

"Hi, Babby," I said as I kissed her. "We don't get to see enough of you. Have you even met the Munchkin?" Rufus was across the room, giggling away, already under Jerry's spell.

"No," she said. "But let's fix that."

"Rufus," I said, "this is Barbara Jenkins, Ms. Lawson's wife."

"Call me Babby," she said, and she gave him a big kiss. Rufus was obviously enchanted. So far, so good. And then the doorbell rang to announce our final guest. I was expecting a boy Rufie's age, but instead I opened the door to discover a man, no more than thirty, medium height, with dark good looks and a radiant smile.

Rufus ran over and greeted our guest. "This is my Uncle Oliver, and this is Mr. Kashani, my science teacher." We said our how-do-you-dos. I liked his handshake very much.

"Please call me Rick," he said. And he handed me a bottle of wine.

"Ollie," I said. "Not necessary, but thank you," I added, indicating the wine.

"Thank *you* for letting me come. Rufus said he told you New York is new to me, and I really don't know anyone. This is a great apartment," he said.

"Thank you. I'm glad you're here, Rick. I'll bet Rufus will take your coat." As Rufus took the coat and prepared to whisk it away to my bedroom, I shot him a look that said, "Aren't you the mysterious one!" His response was pure Jerry. It shouldn't have been a surprise. I had made that bed, after all.

It was a delightful evening, if I do say so myself. The food was just fine, and there was plenty of it—considering the adult appetite I hadn't planned for. And I was pleased to see that Rick did indeed have a healthy appetite, which I always find attractive. Everyone began to head home just before 10:00. It was a school night, after all. Truly. Rick was the last to leave. Rufus offered to get Rick's coat but said he had to go the bathroom first. Rufus was obviously stalling, to give Rick and me time alone. I didn't mind.

As Rick and I walked to my room to retrieve his coat from my bed, Rick said, "Thank you, Ollie, for a lovely evening. May I phone you some time?"

"Of course," I said, and I gave him my number. I wanted to kiss Rick. Very much. He had a very kissy mouth. I doubted he'd have turned me down. But I couldn't bring myself to kiss a man, in my bedroom, while Rufus was nearby. It felt—wrong? Irresponsible? Selfish? Instead, I smiled at Rick, embraced him warmly, and told him I would look forward to his call. I helped him on with his coat, and we headed for the front door. Rufus resurfaced in time to say good night, and Rick was on his way.

"Can your old uncle give a party, or what?" I asked.

"Well done, Uncle Ollie. How much cleanup do we have to do tonight?"

"Just enough so the roaches don't take over the rest. Don't worry about it. You need your sleep. Let's see what we can do in fifteen minutes, and then it's off to bed with you." We started in. And while we were organizing the leftovers, I said, "I like Mr. Kashani."

"He's a good guy. And a good teacher."

"Why didn't you tell me you invited an adult, when you knew I was expecting a classmate?" I asked.

Rufus could tell that was a serious question, and so he considered his reply: "I wasn't sure you'd agree if I told you I was inviting him."

"You're probably right," I said. "But why? Why did you want to invite Mr. Kashani to our home?"

"Because he's nice, and he's smart, and he's lonely. Like you."

"For your information, little man," I said. "I haven't been lonely for even a second since you showed up. Thanks for your concern, but you're not quite nine years old and suddenly you're a matchmaker? I don't think so. I don't think that's the way it works." It was probably because he was tired, but Rufus started to look a little weepy. I grabbed him up into my arms and said, "I love you, Rufus. Go, brush your teeth. Then call me and I'll tuck you in. And I'll sing you that Bette Midler song you like so much—the one with the dirty lyrics." I put him down, and he ran off to his room.

Jesus Fucking Christ! I thought. *What have I gotten myself into? This kid is smarter than I am. How can I stay a jump ahead of him?* I did some cleanup. I tucked Rufus in. I sang—very briefly and very badly—and then I headed to my room to unwind with a tall cognac. I'd have been more than ready to retreat from the day's events, except that I couldn't quite get Rick out of my brain. A science teacher. Single. Lonely. Hot as Hell. Hmmm. But since I didn't have Rick in my arms, and I didn't have enough knowledge of his body to construct a proper fantasy, I simply bade him good night and settled into the arms of Morpheus.

Chapter Ten

Was I looking forward to Rick's call? Of course! He phoned the next day to say thank you, again, for the dinner invitation. He also told me Natural History had a temporary show, closing soon, that Rufus and I both might find interesting. And would we maybe want to meet him there on Sunday afternoon? Definitely yes, I assured him. And we agreed on a time and place. I wasn't sure if it was butterflies or dinosaurs or minerals or what. But I was stoked. And Natural History was Rufus's favorite museum. So I knew it would go well.

On Sunday afternoon, Rick was waiting for us at the museum entrance off 80th Street. He greeted Rufus with a handshake, and then he greeted me with a kiss on both cheeks. Rick had already bought tickets for the three of us. "We have timed tickets for the show," Rick said. "But after that, there's a film for kids that lasts about forty minutes, if you want to see it, Rufus."

"Sure," Rufus said. And we headed into the museum. I loved the warmth of Rick's greeting. I studied his face—as much as possible—as we waited in line. I decided Rick was even handsomer than I remembered—even without candlelight. The show was about climate change, and it was a real eye opener. I was glad we hadn't missed it. Afterward, we walked Rufus to the movie theater and left him in the care of the museum staff while Rick and I went to the café.

We got our coffees and found a table. With all the other museumgoers around us, I still felt as if Rick and I were alone. I liked the feeling. "Tell me about you," I said.

Rick smiled his effortless smile—revealing exceptionally beautiful teeth—and began his story. "My parents left Iran when I was three. They didn't trust the new regime, so they decided to get out while they could. They chose DC. Dad has a business—carpets, wouldn't you know it? Actually, I can tell you that the rugs in your living room are quite fine. In the bedroom? Nice. But I could find you better ones." Rick flashed that wonderful grin of his. I melted.

"They named me Reza. After the Shah? I'm not sure. They won't say. But after I got to America, I felt the need of a new name. I probably hadn't yet seen *CASABLANCA* too many times, at that age. But I decided I wanted to be Rick. My parents didn't fight me. They were reinventing themselves, after all. They let me choose. And that was done. They spoke to me in Farsi while I was growing up. I began to answer them in English. It's the immigrant story. It's so typical. I never really learned Farsi—and I certainly can't read or write it—but I understand much of it, when I hear it.

"I went to Georgetown, and after graduation I got a job with the Smithsonian—an entry-level position at Air and Space. Then they moved me to Natural History, which I loved. And that's where I was until last fall. I like DC. Very much. I just reached a point where I didn't want to live there anymore. My partner left me for a good job in San Francisco. I almost followed him. He invited me. But I suppose I sensed that our affair had run its course. We had been happy together. Marcus is a lovely man. You'd like him, Ollie. Everyone does. He's a charmer. But I couldn't do it. I couldn't move to San Francisco with him. I let him go. And everything else in my life began to feel as empty as my bed. That's when I got the offer to teach, in New York, and I said yes immediately. I was working on programs for young people at the museum, so I was already a teacher, more or less. I never thought of myself as impetuous, but I certainly made some quick decisions this year."

"Good for you, Rick!" I said. "Where are you staying?"

"I found something near school. It's hardly more than a room, but you know what rents are like. My parents offered to subsidize me—a little—the first year. I took them up on it. I'll find something more permanent. I'm not going to rush it."

"No, that's wise. The right situation will come along when it does, and not a moment sooner."

"What about you, Ollie? I don't really know anything about you," Rick said, "except that you're handsome and you're a good father." I gave him the bare bones version of my past, with an emphasis on Louisa and Rufus—so he could understand how my new family came to be. "Rufus is such a bright kid," he said. "All kids astound me—especially New York City kids—but Rufus is exceptional. I'm glad you understand the kind of enrichment he needs. And the love he needs. I think with you and the school behind him, he'll soar."

"From your lips to God's ears," I said. "Rick, will you have dinner with me one night this week?"

"Of course. I was just about to ask the same question. How about Wednesday?

"Perfect," I said. "Have you been to Calisto? It's the best Mexican in the neighborhood."

"No, I haven't. Sounds great. Should we meet there about 7:00?"

"I'll text you the address," I said. "Rick, I'm looking forward to spending some time with you."

"Yes, Ollie. I'm looking forward, too." We finished our coffee and headed to the theater to collect Rufus. The three of us left the museum and headed down Central Park West. Rick peeled off two blocks north of my building. We said our thank-yous and good-byes, and then Rufus and I headed home.

"Did you and Mr. Kashani have a good time?" Rufus asked, as I let us into the apartment.

"Yes, nosey body. He's a nice guy. I like him very much. Is that what you want to know?" I asked.

"Good," Rufus said. "I'm really hungry. What's for supper?"

"That's what I was just about to ask you. You're cooking tonight, correct?"

"Sure, Uncle Ollie. I'm making my famous grilled cheese sandwiches. Coming right up."

"Oh, that's a shame," I said. "I'm not in the mood for cheese tonight. What if I reheat the lentil soup for us?"

"Even better," Rufus said. "I'll set the table." I had a nice little flutter going on in my heart whenever I thought of Rick. Which was often. I also told myself it was only a dinner date. Surely that was all it would be. Yes?

On Wednesday evening, as I was walking Rufus to Jerry's, I said to him, "Rufie, please don't tell anyone at school that I'm having dinner with Mr. Kashani."

"Why?" he asked.

"That's right. Ask the tough questions. Because professional and personal don't always mix so easily. Trust me. Don't give anyone a reason to think that you're getting special treatment because your teacher is friendly with your parent. And don't give anyone a reason to wonder whether or not Mr. Kashani is entirely honest."

"I think I get it," he said. "I just want you two to be friends."

"Yes. Well, we *are* friends. Thank you for that. But just be careful, Rufie. And have a good time with your Uncle Jerry." I headed for the restaurant. Calisto is a welcoming place. We had margaritas and a wonderful gratin of *huitlacoche* and fresh cheese to start. I had eaten black corn fungus in Mexico, and it never tastes exactly the same outside of that country. But it was close enough. Rick was just as appealing as he had been at our last meeting. Maybe more so. We spent a fair bit of our time together just gazing into each other's eyes.

As our dinner was ending, Rick said, "Ollie, will you come to my place? It isn't much, but it's nearby."

"Of course," I said. "I was hoping for an invitation." That was the truth. I had been warming to the possibility for the last two hours. In fact, I had to try to arrange my erection in an inconspicuous way before we left the restaurant. Thank God for long sweaters. As promised, Rick's apartment was only a few blocks away. He invited me in. And, as promised, it was small. But functional. My only real interest was Rick's bed, and that was waiting patiently for us.

First kisses are always special to me. Rick's kiss was warm and generous. I loved it. "I've wanted to kiss you for a week now," I said. "But even in my best fantasies it wasn't *that* good."

"Agreed," Rick said. "Oliver, please come to my bed. I want you." I needed no other encouragement. We peeled off our winter garb and slipped between the sheets—but not before I got a good look at Rick's body. He was trim and toned. Not muscular, exactly, but perfectly masculine. And his skin had an inviting softness like velvet beneath my touch. I wrapped myself around Rick and savored his warmth. I drew in his scent. Deeply. Rick awakened all the desire that been sleeping in me.

We had a lovely first encounter. We smiled a lot. We kissed a lot. We explored. I liked everything I discovered, equally. Rick's hands were just as beautiful as his feet and his limbs and his shoulders and his chest and his ears and his throat and his mouth and his butt and his ample dick. I wanted every part of him. I tried to take my time and enjoy them all. He seemed to feel the same way about me.

I was a generalist, to begin with. Later, I specialized. I focused on Rick's ass and tried my best to honor him with my attentions. I buried my face between his legs. I was in my happy place. Rick seemed to go there, too. I don't know how long I was down there. I could have moved in, I think. There didn't seem to be any rush. But eventually I felt the need to vary the diet. "Rick, will you let me . . .?

"Anything, Oliver," he said. "Whatever you want." And what I wanted at that moment was to be as deep inside Rick as I could manage. I moved my body into position to top him. I lifted his head from his pillow and kissed him. I was still kissing him when I pressed forward, very gently. Rick's body hesitated at first, but then he accepted me. I was in. There's something so intimate about accessing another man's interior. Fellatio can be as casual as a hand-shake. But going inside? Not so different from holding another man's heart in my hands, I always thought. I began to feel a bit awed. I also felt warm and wonderful.

I moved slowly and carefully inside Rick. I wanted to give him pleasure, and I also wanted to delay the inevitable as long as possible. It's never long enough, but I stayed inside Rick as long as I could. He could tell I was getting close. And then we both shouted, "Good God!" in unison. After we had recovered from the experience a little, Rick rolled over and showed me that he came, too! I felt proud that I had facilitated it, but I also felt sad that I had missed seeing it—his first with me. I vowed not to miss out on anything like that again, if indeed we would be having any agains. I hoped so, but?

"Ollie, that was incredible," Rick said. "I've never done that before." I looked a bit shocked, I suppose. "No, not that," he said. "I meant I've never had an orgasm along with the beautiful man inside me. That's one I'll never forget. Thank you, Ollie."

"Don't be silly," I said. "Thank *you*, Rick. I sup-pose I should head home. It's a school night, after all. But I don't want to leave."

"No," Rick said. "I don't want you to leave. But will you come back?"

"As often as I'm invited," I said. "But, I don't know, Rick. Is this appropriate? Going to bed with Rufus's teacher."

"I don't see a conflict of interest. We both want what's best for him. And if we also enjoy each other's company, I can't see a problem there."

"I hope you're right," I said. "Rick, I don't know what to say. You've got me thinking how much I want to make love to you. Every day would be nice. But we've only just met, and life's a little more complicated than that. I'm trying to do the right things for Rufus."

"And succeeding."

"Thanks for that," I said. "So, what do you think we should do next?"

"I think we should get on with our lives. You have to pick Rufus up at Jerry's and take him home. I have to finalize a lesson plan for tomorrow. Could we meet on the weekend?"

"Yes, please," I said. "Text me. Rufus and I both love being with you. Brunch, maybe? And then something after? You choose."

"Thanks, Ollie. That was beautiful. I'm still light-headed from it. You're a gorgeous man."

"Ditto," I said. I kissed Rick, deeply, and then I bundled up and headed out into the real world. When I collected Rufus, I sensed he knew that Rick and I had made love—as much as he could understand such things at his age. But he was silent about it. "How's your Uncle Jerry?" I asked.

"He's fine. He said I should tell you that you owe him big time, and that he's expecting some gold jewelry for his birthday."

"He can expect all he wants, but he'll get the usual dinner and a card. Maybe I'll throw in a bottle of champagne this year." I asked, "What do you think, little man?"

"I think Uncle Jerry deserves a trip to Paris. He suggested it."

"May I come along? Or will it be just the two of you?" I asked.

"We decided you should come with us. If you want to. If you wouldn't miss Mr. Kashani too much."

"I'll think about it, smart-ass. Meanwhile, the only place we're going tonight is to bed. Let's get you home." And that's what we did.

Chapter Eleven

Rick phoned me the next day and said, "I'd love to cook for you. I'm a decent Persian cook, but I can't do much at my place, as you saw. I can make an omelet and warm up takeout. That's about it."

"What if we cooked at my house?" I asked. "If I shop for ingredients, will you come over and show Rufus and me how to do it?"

"Don't you think shopping for ingredients is half the fun? But I have no idea where to find some of the more exotic ones, like dried limes."

"Not to worry," I said. "I'll take you shopping at Kalustyan. They have everything. This weekend, maybe?

"I'd like that," Rick said. "Choose a day."

"Saturday, I think. We could meet there. It's an Indian food neighborhood, really. Why don't we meet for a late breakfast at an Indian vegetarian restaurant?"

"Perfect."

"And then we can shop afterward. This sounds like fun, Rick," I said.

"Yes, Ollie," he said. "Just being with you would be enough, but a whole day of shopping and cooking and eating will be a special treat. Until Saturday, then."

Bruce K Beck

"Until Saturday," I said. By the time I had ended the call, I was feeling a bit flushed. "What's going on here?" I asked myself. "Are you trying to fall in love with Rick? Because you're doing a good job of it." I was, of course. But I told myself I had no time for such things. Wasn't it bad enough that Will had me up in the air? Surely I didn't need another romantic entanglement. Did I?

I started a new project that week. It was a novel—supposedly being written by a celebrity who was "inspired by" a real event. Fortunately for him, he's a better actor than writer. The notes the publisher sent me were difficult to parse. But the premise was interesting. I decided I could turn it into a good, suspenseful read. I welcomed the distraction. Other than that, it was daily life. Will cancelled our Friday because he had promised Sam he'd attend a game at Sam's school. Even a month earlier, I'd have been deeply sad about it. But as things were, I shrugged it off and got on with my routine.

Rufus was excited about Saturday, too. We met Rick at Chennai Garden at 11:00, as they were opening. I love dosas. Potato is my favorite. Idlis are nice, too, but less interesting texture-wise. We ordered lots of dishes. It was all good. Rufus seemed pleased with the little explosions of flavor in the mouth. I was even more pleased with the chance to sit next to Rick again. We ate. We smiled. We talked. We drank good black tea. And then we headed to the spice shop on Lexington.

I had laid in staples the day before. Rick sent me a list, and so I had my butcher cut up lamb shoulder for stewing. Rufus went with me to Fairway after the gym on Friday, where we bought onions and scallions and cilantro and four huge bunches of parsley. I decided on canned red kidney beans so we wouldn't have to worry about getting them tender but not mushy. I already had vegetable oil and olive oil in the house, of course. And the usual spices. So at Kalustyan we bought dried Persian limes—whole and powdered, both—plus saffron, basmati rice, ground turmeric, and a small bag of ground fenugreek seed.

Rick had already told me we would probably not find fresh fenugreek leaves. So instead we could use a pinch of ground seed plus extra parsley. He learned that workaround from his mother. It sounded reasonable to me. We headed home with our treasures. Once we had unpacked and organized our exotics, I began to wonder how we would spend the rest of the afternoon. We didn't really need to start cooking until maybe 4:00.

"I'm going to take a nap," Rufus said. "I think you should, too."

"Thanks for the advice, little man." I said. "I think you're right." Rufus headed off to his room—with his phone, of course—while I led Rick to mine. And I closed the door behind us. "I don't know, Rick. I don't know if I can make love to you while Rufus is just down the hall. But I'm going to try."

"Good," Rick said. "I have every faith in you." I undressed him. His body was even more exciting in the diffused daylight of my bedroom than it had seemed at his apartment our first time together.

Bruce K Beck

As I knelt before him, removing his shoes and his jeans, I said, "God, Rick! You are so beautiful I can hardly stand it."

"You took the words right out of my mouth, Ollie," he said. "Please come to bed and let me hold you." I did, of course. I stripped and joined Rick. We held each other so tenderly that I felt complete, just as we were. My raging hard-on mirrored Rick's, and yet neither of us needed any athletic expressions of our passion. We simply embraced. Quietly. Closely. Small movements were enough to achieve big results. Before long we bathed each other in sweet pearlescence.

We continued to hold each other. "I've fallen in love with you, Ollie," Rick said.

"Now who's taking the words out of whose mouth?" I asked. "Rick, what are we going to do about this?"

"Besides cooking *qormeh sabzi* together and having a good dinner tonight?" he asked.

"Besides cooking . . . *whatever* together and having a good dinner tonight," I said. "Rick, I want to get this right. I don't know if I can care for Rufus and still have enough of me left to offer a beautiful man. I couldn't bear to shortchange you. You deserve 100%."

"Please let me worry about that, Ollie," Rick said. "Whatever you have to give will be enough. I'm not high maintenance. I'm very practical, really. And very much in love." I tightened my embrace. We were silent for a while, and then we got up, cleaned up some, and put our clothes back on. Was it as if nothing had happened? No, it was much better than that. We had shared a natural expression of our feelings for each other, and it had been deeply satisfying.

Dinner was delicious, as I assumed it would be. Rufus seemed to be having a good time. My kitchen was unusually active, of course—and aromatic. And Rick was so at ease with browning the onions and the meat and chopping all the herbs finely. It was a chance for Rufus to see how a real cook does it. He seemed fascinated with the process, as well as the sounds and the smells. We spent such a relaxed evening together, it was almost enough to relieve my fears about the new development on the romance front. Almost.

Will phoned me the next week. "I'm really sorry, Ollie, but I won't be able to see you this Friday. Again," he said. "It's complicated. I'll try to tell you everything I know about it. The problem is, I have no idea where it's going." He sounded as if he was about to hyperventilate.

"Will," I said. "Don't torture yourself. Just tell me what's happening."

"Yes, Ollie. You're right, of course. Jennifer called me. She wants to come back. She wants to move back in and be my wife and Sam's full-time mother again. It's the last thing I could have imagined, and yet it happened."

"What did you say?" I asked.

"After I picked myself up off the floor?"

"Exactly," I said.

"I told her I needed time to consider her request. I told her I had to speak to Sam about it. I asked her to wait for my reply. She agreed. That was on Saturday. I feel like I'm in limbo now."

"What will you do?" I asked.

"I haven't talked to Sam about it yet. I can't deny him the chance of a reconciliation, and yet I couldn't bear to see him abandoned again. I never stopped loving Jennifer. I could welcome her back into my life and into my bed. I could do it. But *only* if it's the perfect situation for Sam. I don't know, Ollie. I don't know what to do."

"I don't envy you, Will," I said. "But I know you'll figure it out. You're smart, and you have a kind heart. You'll make it work, whichever way it goes."

"Sam comes first, but then there's you, Ollie. Way ahead of Jennifer. I want what's best for you. Don't think I'm not holding you close to my heart every moment while I'm trying to navigate this mess."

"Never mind me, Will," I said. "You have enough complications in your life. I think we have to hit the pause button on our friendship. I think you need to focus on the people who are closest to you. And I'm not one of them. Thank you for thinking I could be, but that doesn't seem to be where we're headed." Wow, that hurt! But I said it. And I meant it.

"Jesus, Ollie! I couldn't love you more if I tried," Will said. "But I think you're right, as always. May I call you, now and then?"

"If there's something you need—if I can help in any way—then you *must* call me. Otherwise? I don't think so. I can't see . . . I can't just . . . I can't be that kind of friend to you. Right now. Maybe in the future."

"Of course," Will said. "I do love you, Ollie. Please don't hate me."

"I couldn't," I said. And that was that. I didn't, of course. I didn't hate Will for the situation he found himself in. I didn't hate Carlos for the turn *his* life took. I've known for a lot of years now that shit happens. And it's up to me to get on with life. I had Rufus to consider. I had my work. And, of course, I had Rick. Maybe. Didn't I?

_________ *Chapter Twelve*

I was sitting at my desk Monday morning. The new novel was going well. I was calculating the best way to draw readers into the thickening plot when my phone rang. The caller ID told me it was Carlos. I gave it two more rings while I decided if I wanted to answer. I did answer. "Hi, Carly."

"Hi, Ollie. How are you?"

"Well, thanks, and you?"

"I'm good. Ollie, can you believe it's been a year since we saw each other?"

"Yes, actually," I said. "Carly, It's good to hear your voice, but why are you calling me?"

"Yes, well, I wondered if you'll have dinner with me."

"Carly, I always loved having dinner with you," I said, "You know that. But I need more information. Why do you want to see me?"

"Yes, well, it's difficult for me to explain it over the phone. I've always felt that I can tell you anything. When we're together. Will you see me?"

"Not for dinner," I said. "I have a child, now. Louie's child. I'm home most nights. But I'll meet you for breakfast, or something, after I drop Rufus off at school."

"On Wednesday?" he asked.

"Yes," I said.

"Thanks, Ollie. Please text me the time and place. I'll be there." And then we ended the call. Was I feeling a bit off balance? You bet. My writing called to me. I got back to work. I put the idea of Carlos out of my mind—as much as possible.

On Wednesday morning I dropped Rufus off at school as usual, and then I went to meet Carlos at a coffee shop nearby. I was a little early. He was nearly on time. I had a few minutes to think about the situation before he arrived. It made no sense, and so I stopped wondering what to expect and concentrated on the idea of breakfast. I can handle any situation better with a little food in my tummy.

"You look great, Carly," I said. He did, of course. I studied the hunk across the table from me and wondered if he had really been mine for five years.

"So do you, Ollie," he said. "I've missed you." I had no response to that comment.

I said, "Let's order something. They have the usual coffee shop breakfast. The hash browns are especially good here. I'm sort of off potatoes right now, but I don't know how you eat these days."

"I still eat pretty much everything. Hash browns sound good." We ordered. We sipped our coffee. I waited. Carlos seemed in no hurry. Our food arrived right away. I never understood how those short-order guys can produce a breakfast plate with such speed. But they do. We ate. I had almost forgotten how quickly Carlos ate, yet with elegance and obvious enjoyment. The waitress removed our plates. We refocused on our coffee cups. And still I waited.

A few minutes later Carlos said, "I meant it when I said I've missed you, Ollie. That's why I phoned. I think I made a big mistake last year. I want to come back. If you'll have me."

"Jesus, Carly!" I said. "How could you do this to me? I think it's cruel."

"Ollie, you know I never stopped loving you. And I think you still love me. I think we belong together, if you can forgive me. I was wrong. I know that now. I'd do anything to make it right again."

"Thanks for getting to the point, Carly," I said. "I'm too shocked to have a reply for you. I won't say no, but . . . give me a few days to consider it. My life is more complicated now. There are other people involved. It's not so simple as our love for each other used to be. I'll phone you when I figure it out." It *was* complicated. I thought of Rufus, of course. Most of all, I thought of Rick. I even thought of Will, though surely that relationship had ended. Hadn't it?

"Thanks, Ollie," he said. "I'll wait for your call. I know you'll do the right thing." I wasn't so sure. We rose to leave. Carlos embraced me very sweetly. He certainly knew how to push my buttons. He kissed me on the cheek, and we parted. I was feeling a little wobbly. Fresh air helped. I walked home slowly, trying to make some sense of the last half hour. When I got back to my desk, I focused on my work and dismissed the rest. More or less.

That afternoon, I picked Rufus up from school, as always, and we headed to the gym. Afterward, I walked him home, gave him a snack, and sat him down at the kitchen table to start his homework. Rick phoned me. We hadn't spoken since the evening before, but he was most certainly fresh in my mind. "The strangest thing happened," Rick began. *He thinks* his *life is strange,* I thought. "I got a call from Marcus. He's coming to town next week. His office is sending him to work on a project here for about a month. If it goes well, they'll transfer him to New York. He asked to stay with me. I told him the apartment is too small, and I couldn't see the two of us bumping into each other for a month. I didn't tell him about you. I'll do that when I see him. Isn't that weird, Ollie?"

"Yes, Rick," I said, "but it's a weird day. I have some strangeness of my own to tell you about. Can we get together on the weekend?"

"Of course," Rick said. "Saturday or Sunday?"

"How about both?" I asked.

"Even better," Rick said. "I could make a plan for Saturday, and you could think of something for Sunday."

"Perfect," I said. I did *not* say, "I love you." Rufus was right there, and I couldn't get the words out. But I thought them. I hoped that was a start, anyway. I went to my desk and knocked out a plan for the next chapter. And then I put together some supper for Rufus and me. "Jesus!" I said to myself. "Who declared this ex month?"

I took my time considering Carly's request. We had been so happy together. For how many years—

until we weren't anymore? I was happy right up until the day Carlos told me he was leaving. I can't speak for him. "I can't do this anymore," is strong stuff. It must have been building for a while. Never mind what I saw and didn't see. That situation was mostly about Carlos. And now the decision at hand was mostly about me.

I could have done it. I could have invited him back into my life. Our lives entwined—our hearts and our bodies entwined—it was all so familiar. So comfortable. So satisfying. I could have done it. And yet there were so many other factors to consider. On a primal level, there was the possibility of his abandoning me again. It was a possibility, after all. It had happened once before. Could I survive a repeat? Could I take the risk? Maybe. Life is risky. I've known for a long time that I can't just swim in the shallows.

I considered, at length, how Rufus figured in this. I decided that he would be very pleased to see me happily partnered. I decided that he and Carlos would learn to love each other. And I knew the apartment was plenty big enough to absorb another family member. In other words, I decided that Rufus was not really a factor in my decision after all. That was a bit of a shock. And yet it relieved an uncomfortable pressure that had been building in my brain.

I also thought about Will. Of course. I decided the pause in our friendship was permanent, no matter how his living situation shook out. I let go of him. Completely. Perhaps. For the first time? Perhaps. I had gone to the well and refilled my cup. I had no room for emptiness. I got on with it. When I began to consider Rick, everything felt different, immediately. Was it the fluttery excitement of newness? Or

was it something deeper? I decided to let myself off
the hook—until the weekend, anyway.

Chapter Thirteen

On Saturday morning Rick met us for breakfast, and then we walked across the Park to Fifth Avenue. It wasn't really spring yet, but there was a scent of anticipation in the air that made my sap rise. Or was it being with Rick? We walked up the avenue to the Met Museum. There were several interesting temporary exhibits, as always. I wanted Rufus to see the one about religious art from Congo. Rick and I wanted to see it as well, of course. It was stunning. We spent another hour or so with my favorites, and Rick's favorites, from the permanent collection. We agreed on the beauty of the Whistlers and the Goyas and the Van Dykes and the Vermeers.

We stopped for a coffee in the café with the big windows onto the Park. Rufus yawned dramatically. "I need a nap," he said. "And it looks like you need a nap, too."

"In that case, little man, I guess we'd better get you home," I said. And that's what we did. We headed back through the park, stopping to admire the Bethesda Fountain this time. "Didn't I tell you it's beautiful in all seasons?" I asked Rufus. "Wait till you see it in a month or so." Rick and I held hands as we enjoyed another first time. And then the three of us walked silently back to Central Park West.

When I let us into the apartment, Rufus bounded toward his room. He stopped, turned, and said, "I'm so sleepy, I figure maybe two hours."

"Okay, Rufe," I said. "I'll make sure you don't miss dinner." And he was off. Rick and I headed to my room, and I shut the door behind us, carefully, of course. It was such a treat to be alone with Rick again. I kissed him. Deeply. He responded. We slipped out of our clothes and got into my bed. "Welcome back, Rick. I've missed you."

"Tell me, Ollie," he said. "I don't like it when we're apart."

"Ditto," I said. "Rick, you're such a sweet man. I could build my life around you."

"Ollie, please make love to me. We can talk later. We can talk on the phone. But this time together is rare. Let's not waste it." We didn't, of course. I wrapped myself around Rick as tightly as I dared. I rolled my body on top of his and kissed him as if I wanted our mouths to merge—as indeed I did. I wanted every part of Rick. I wanted the warmth of his embrace as much as anything else. I couldn't quite decide where to go next. I'm often a take-charge kind of guy. That Saturday afternoon? Not so much.

I think Rick sensed my indecision. He said, "Ollie, you're so tense. Roll over. Let me see if I can apply some ancient Persian massage techniques. You need some body work." I did, of course—need body work *and* agree to roll over. Rick straddled my back and started in on my shoulders. I loved the weight of his body on mine. I loved the strength of his hands, working my tightened muscles. I loved the fact that we were together, and that he wanted to bring me relaxation. I loved *him*, of course. That was the major factor.

Rick worked his way down my back, bringing me pleasure all along the path. When he got to my butt cheeks, he took special care to knead them into submission. When he said, "Ollie, may I?" I said, "Do it." And he did. He placed his full weight on top of my body—which was thrilling enough—and then he kissed me and took the plunge. I accepted his dick as effortlessly as if we had been lovers always. I received him into my body almost as easily as I had welcomed him into my heart.

Rick was gentle and respectful. He was also strong and reassuringly in control. I gave him my body to do with as he chose. I trusted him to use it well. And he did. He seemed to know exactly what would bring me the most pleasure. I wasn't always certain who was doing what to whom. And, of course, that's pretty much what the best lovemaking is all about, isn't it? I can be a vessel. I can go into surrender-mode. I can submit to a man who demands submission. It can be a dreamy state, given the right circumstances. But I prefer to be a partner in the experience. And with Rick, I was.

"Jesus, Rick, how did you do that?" I asked, when we had recovered a bit.

"Ancient Persian magic," he said. "I know a few more spells, if you're interested."

"Yes, please, all of them. One at a time, maybe? All at once might kill me. Rick . . ." He stopped my prattle with a kiss.

"Ollie," he said, "I've never been this happy in my life. Could we maybe see if we can sustain it? I can't be certain, of course, what you want. But I want you, and us, together."

"Yes, Rick," I said. "That's what I want, too." We relaxed into a nap-like state. For a while. It was delicious lying in my bed in the afternoon sunlight with a promise of spring to it; in the arms of a precious man who had declared his love for me. Eventually, we stirred. "Tell me about Marcus," I said.

"Yes, well, I think I told you he gets into town on Monday. And he'll be here the rest of the month, at least. I'd like you to meet him, Ollie. He's a special man."

"If you love him, then he'd have to be," I said.

"He's great looking, I think. He's . . . well, you'll see. He's kind, and honest, and I thought we were in it for the duration. But when it was time for him to move on, it was time for me, too."

"But he asked to stay in your apartment. No?"

"Yes, Ollie, he asked to stay with me. People need a place to stay. I assumed his company has a budget for lodgings. If he had needed shelter, I'd have probably said yes. But as it was, I said no. You seem to be suggesting more than I read into the situation."

"Rick, don't be silly," I said. "This story has 'I want you back' written all over it. I have a little experience of such things. Recent experience. Carlos wants to come back to me. He told me so, Wednesday morning."

"Ollie, what did you say?"

"I told him I didn't have an answer, and that he'd have to wait until I did have one. If he asked me *tomorrow* morning, I'd simply tell him that I'm so in love with you that I couldn't possibly consider anyone else in my future. But on Wednesday I started to think about Rufus, and Will, and you, of course, believe me. And the past. And it fogged my judgment. I left it flying. I'm not proud of that. I'll fix it. Can you forgive me?"

"For having a past?" Rick asked. "If you can forgive mine."

"Come here, Rick," I said. "Could I just hold you for a hundred years or so?"

"That's all?" he asked. "I want to hold *you* forever. But I'll settle for your terms. I think we can fit a lifetime into whatever years we're granted. Do you really want to grill steaks tonight? Because I think we should go out."

"So smart," I said. "I love smart men. Rick, will you marry me?"

"Ollie, are you serious?"

"Never more so."

"Yes," Rick said. "There's nothing on Earth that could bring me more joy. Yes. Let's do it, Ollie!" We were bubbling with excitement, of course. It would have been delightful to spend the rest of the day in my bed. But we needed to get ourselves up, to think about dinner, to think about Rufus.

"Rick, would you mind if we don't tell anyone about this, for now? There'll be plenty of time to share our news after we've made plans. I'm sure Rufus will be thrilled, but I'm not ready to tell even him. What do you think?"

"I think it's up to you, Ollie," Rick said. "I'm happy to keep this our secret, if that's what you want. Also, it'll make it easier for you to back out without having to make a bunch of explanations."

"Come here, you," I said. "There will be no cold feet. I love you so much that I've never been more certain of anything in my life. Let's tell Rufus. He deserves to know. After all, it was his idea in the first place." Rick kissed me. We held each other for a while and smiled a lot. Then we got up and pulled ourselves together.

When we resurfaced from my room, Rufus was waiting for us—sitting in the kitchen and playing a game on his phone. When I told him our news, Rufus let out a joyous whoop that was loud enough to be heard all the way to the Bethesda Fountain. He grabbed us both and danced us around the kitchen. He was bouncing with joy. "What do you think, little man?" I asked.

"I think you finally grew up, Uncle Ollie. I'm so proud of you."

"Thanks, Rufe, for your vote of confidence. Rick and I haven't really talked about wedding plans. We haven't gotten that far. What do you think, Rick. Should we marry in June? After the school term ends?"

"Perfect," Rick said. "Yes, mid-June. I like that."

"It just occurred to me: That's the ideal time for an outdoor wedding in the City. Have you been to the Conservatory Gardens?"

"No," Rick said.

"I'll take you there in a month or two, when the cherry blossoms peak."

"I'd like that," Rick said.

Rufus asked him, "After you're married, what will I call you?"

"How about Rick?" he answered.

"Rufe," I said. "You two can work that out between yourselves. But don't forget that until the end of the school term, he's Mr. Kashani."

"Yes, Uncle Ollie. I understand."

"Let's get some dinner," I said. "Let's celebrate. Let's pig out on pasta." And that's what we did.

Rick came back to the apartment with Rufus and me. I said to him, "Rick, will you stay over tonight? There's no point in your going home when we have a morning plan. You've never slept in my bed. I want you there." I called to Rufus and asked, "Rufie, how loud is my snoring?"

"Kind of like a taxi horn. But don't worry, Mr. Kashani. I got used to it, the weeks I slept on the chaise."

"Thanks for your input, little man." I said. "I think we should get ready for bed." And that's what we did. Rufus went off to change into his pajamas and brush his teeth, while Rick and I poured ourselves a nightcap. Then I went and tucked Rufus in. I kissed him on the forehead and said, "Sleep tight, precious boy." He knew, of course, that I was thanking him for pushing me toward happiness—toward completing our family.

Rick and I sat at the kitchen table for a while, nursing our cognac. We smiled a lot. I said, "Rick,"

"Yes, Ollie."

"Do you really want me? Do you really want us?"

"Ollie, I love you," he said. "And so I'll forgive a certain number of stupid questions. Ollie, I've wanted you since the first moment we met. I'm not stupid. I can assess quality rather quickly. I knew from our first handshake that you were the man for me. I just didn't know if *you* knew it. I didn't know if I should come on strong or wait for you to figure it

out at your own pace. I think I did some of each.
But we're here, however we did it. Please don't question it."

"No, Rick, I won't question us. Ever. But I do
have a question for *you*. Will you move in? I want
you here. I want us to have every minute together
that we can."

"It's tempting, Ollie," he said. "I want us to be
together as much as you do. But I think we should
wait. Until the end of the school term. It's only a few
months. I'm not worried about appearances, but I
don't want Rufus in the middle of something uncomfortable at school. I told you I don't see any conflict
of interest. But I also don't want to ask for trouble.
The school is invested in progressive educational values. Social values? Maybe not so much. What do
you think?"

"I think you're perfect," I said. "I'm not, unfortu-
nately. I think I was supposed to make a plan for
tomorrow, but I haven't done it. Will you help?"

"With pleasure," Rick said. "Why don't we have
coffee and a piece of toast when we get up and then
head to Chinatown for dim sum?"

"Excellent!" I said. "Rufus loves to show off his
skill with chopsticks. And then?"

"And then why don't we just see where the day
takes us?" I couldn't imagine anything better.

Chapter Fourteen

Rick sleeping in my bed felt perfectly natural to me. I wanted him beside me always. I wanted to share his embrace and feel the warmth of his body next to mine. I hated getting out of bed on Sunday morning. But at least I knew I would have Rick with me the rest of the day. Rufus got up before we did, so there was the perfume of freshly brewed coffee to greet Rick and me as we wandered into the kitchen. I sliced some bread. Rufus toasted it for us. I had bought some Irish butter recently that was full of flavor. And some Scottish marmalade. We were ready to face the new day.

We took the C train to Canal Street and walked east to Bowery, then south to Chatham Square. My favorite dim sum parlor was packed with people, but the wait for a table—or rather, three seats at a table—was only about ten minutes. I've always thought three people for dim sum is ideal, considering how many of the little plates have three pieces on them. We ate too much very good food—I even got Rufus to try a chicken foot, and Rick and I discovered our shared fondness for tripe. Then we headed out into the noontime sun.

It was such a beautiful day that we decided to walk for a while. We headed west on Canal Street, and then north until we ended up on Gansevoort

Street. After a visit to the new Whitney Museum—none of us had seen it yet—we decided to take a walk on the High Line. It was a lovely afternoon. We returned home, and I grilled steaks for our dinner. I began to feel sad, knowing our perfect day was about to end. I didn't give in to sadness, however. I refused to waste the happiness of even one of our minutes together.

Rufus went to bed, and I gave Rick a goodbye kiss. "I had a thought," Rick said. "We haven't really discussed the subject of our exes. We have to deal with them, and soon. So why don't we organize a dinner party? For the four of us. In a restaurant. That could be a very civilized way to handle our news. I'm sure you'll like Marcus, and I'm dying to meet Carlos."

"I think that's perfect—rather like yourself," I said. "Let me call Jerry and see when he's free to take Rufus. And then we can go from there." And that's what we did.

I was not looking forward to our Thursday dinner, but I knew I couldn't duck my responsibility to Carlos. I had promised him an answer, and he deserved an explanation. The four of us gathered at 7:00 at a restaurant in the neighborhood. I was rather nervous about the whole thing, but we got on with the business of introductions and small talk. Rick was right—Marcus was a charmer. He was also great looking—medium height, red-haired with a beautiful beard. I began to feel quite grateful that Rick chose me over his handsome ex.

I finally took the bull by the horns and announced our engagement. "Ollie, why didn't you tell me last week?" Carlos asked.

"Good question," I answered. "Perhaps I didn't know enough about it at the time. You and I were very much in love, Carlos. I couldn't just dismiss that. Probably I should have told you about Rick when we had breakfast. But I didn't. And so I'm telling you now." Carlos had no reply.

"Rick, why didn't *you* tell *me*?" Marcus asked.

"First of all, Marcus, you didn't ask." Rick said. "You only asked for a place to stay. If you had asked me about my life, I would have told you that I chose Ollie. But you didn't. So, I'm telling you now." Marcus fell silent, too. Just then our food arrived, so that took away some of the gravity of awkward silence. Other than a few polite comments on the quality of the food, we were a quiet bunch.

Over coffee, Carlos asked, "So, Marcus, how do you like San Francisco?"

"Very much," Marcus answered. "I'm not wild about the climate, but it's a beautiful city. Still, I'm hoping this project works out so I can move to New York. I always wanted to live here."

"I was born here, so I don't have a broad base for comparison," Carlos said. "But I've never wanted to live anywhere else. I hope it works out for you." By the time we were putting on our coats to leave the restaurant, the exes were exchanging phone numbers. I looked at Rick and we both tried very hard not to burst out laughing. The good nights were cordial all around.

As I walked Rick to his building, he said, "Well, Ollie, Carlos is even hunkier than I expected. Are you sure you don't want him back?"

"I think it's too late for that," I said. "I think he's fallen under Marcus's spell. No surprise there. Marcus is hot stuff. Are you sure you're ready to give him up?"

"After the wedding, maybe I could have Marcus on the side," Rick said.

"I'm sure that could be arranged, but not if you're planning to marry *me*," I said. I stopped us, right there on the sidewalk, and said, "Rick, I'm quite amazed at how completely I love you. And that you love me, too. I thought life with Carlos was happy—most of the time, anyway—but nothing prepared me for the joy I feel when I'm with you." Rick kissed me deeply. My joy meter went over the top.

"Ollie, thanks for letting me love you," Rick said. "You're a gift. A big, beautiful gift. I'd love to unwrap you. Maybe this weekend?"

"Please," I said. I was feeling buoyant as I walked to Jerry's and collected Rufus. He was quite sleepy, so I carried him the last two blocks home. I was surprised at how much he had grown in just the few months since he entered my life and my heart. I was very much aware of change and unpredictability. I was also aware of how blessed I felt. It was a great feeling.

"The headmaster called me into his office today," Rick said at dinner one night the next week. Rufus had gone out to a movie with Jerry, so Rick and I were alone. "He disapproves of my having a relationship with a student's parent," Rick said. "He didn't actually say I won't be back next term. But that was the implication. They do these things very carefully. I'd guess he got the script for his conversation from his attorney."

"Rick, I'm so sorry," I said. "I'd hoped to spare you this. So much for secrecy." My heart sank. The thought of our love causing Rick pain and professional confusion was chilling to me. "How can I help?" I asked. "What can I do to make up for this?"

"You can love me. And you're doing an excellent job of that, so far."

"Thanks for the positive review. And I'll keep at it." I was saddened by the negativity, but I wasn't all that concerned about the future, really. I knew Rick would find other, probably better work. And I knew that I could carry the family finances. I had my work, the payments Charles and Cynthia sent for Rufus's upkeep, and the earnings on the last of my trust fund—which pretty much covered the monthly maintenance payments on the apartment. Whatever happened, I felt, we could eat and avoid the street. We would be just fine.

"Speaking of positive reviews, I expect I can get one if I leave quietly," Rick said. "That's often how it works, I think. I would prefer *that* to launching public charges of discrimination. I'll go there if necessary. But I hope it won't be. Most of all, I want to spare Rufus the blowback from a scandal. Being a kid is hard enough without public humiliation."

I became a little weepy. I said, "Rick, I've done nothing in my life to deserve you, but fuck it! I'll keep you anyway, as long as you'll have me." Rick and I made love, and then he headed home to his apartment. As soon as he left I felt Rick's absence deeply, but I reminded myself it was temporary. I was coping nicely by the time Jerry brought Rufus home. I hadn't told Jerry yet about Rick's and my engagement. I wasn't sure if Rufus had given it away or not. But of course I would have to tell Jerry, anyway. We had always shared the important things.

"How was the movie?" I asked as Rufus bounded in.

"It was okay," Rufus said. "But Uncle Jerry's stories are better."

"I'll bet they are," I said. "Why don't you get ready for bed?" I suggested. "Jer, how about a nightcap?"

"Sure," he said. I poured his favorite Scotch, and we sat at the kitchen table to savor it, just like two old friends—as indeed we were.

"I have news, dear." I got right to it. "Rick and I are getting married. In June. Will you stand up for me?"

"Ollie, that's fabulous!" Jerry said, and he embraced me. "I saw it coming, I think. I saw the way you and Rick looked at each other at your dinner party. I'm not surprised in the least. And I'm delighted. Of course I'll be your best man."

"I wasn't sure if Rufus told you or not. We were supposed to keep it a secret until Rick sorted out the implications for his future at Rufie's school. But Uncle Jerry is a powerful force. I didn't know if Rufe could keep the secret or not. I'm proud of him."

"As well you should be. I can't believe I've missed another chance."

"Chance at what?" I asked.

"At catching you between husbands," Jerry said.

"Oh, Jerry. You got bored with me—fifteen years ago? Why would today be any different?"

"Ollie, that's not the truth, and you know it. You've never bored me for an instant. I've always wanted you. And I've settled for your friendship because it's what's available. And I'll hold onto it, if I may."

"I do love you, Jerry," I said. "Please don't give up on me. I need you in my life as much as ever."

"Now that that's settled, let me ask what happened to make you decide to let the cat out of the bag?"

Yes, well, the cat got out already, somehow." I said. "Rick was called in on the carpet today. He's done nothing ethically wrong, of course, but the headmaster is displeased with the look of it."

"Any number of things could have happened, don't you think? Probably some parent saw you two together at a school event and surmised a relationship. Some parent with an evil mind and a big mouth. That's often how these things happen," Jerry said. "I see it all the time at work. We're not a very pretty species, Ollie, in case you hadn't noticed."

"Some prettier than others. I'm glad I surround myself only with beauties." Rufus came out of his room to say good night. "I'll be there in a minute to tuck you in," I said. "Just let me say good night to your Uncle Jerry." We embraced.

"I'm so happy for you, Ollie," Jerry said. "May I kiss the bride?"

"That's up to her," I said. "But you can kiss me." And he did kiss me, very sweetly. Did it make me wonder what my life would be if Jerry and I had recombined at some point in recent history? Of course. I decided that life with Jerry would be wonderful, but that life with Rick would be even better. I slept well.

Chapter Fifteen

"Hi, Oliver, it's Priscilla," she said on the phone that Tuesday morning. "I have some good news for you."

"Always welcome. How are you, Prissy? We haven't spoken in a while."

"No, it's been a quiet time on your legal front. But I wanted you to know the judge will hear your adoption petition next week. It's the strongest way for you to have permanent custody, and it looks good."

"Oh, Prissy, thank God! What do we have to do?"

"You'll have to take Rufus out of school that morning, because you both have to appear in court. All the important documents have already been filed. The court knows that Rufus was orphaned by his mother's death and that you are requesting to be the replacement parent. It may seem odd, but the case will be heard in the Surrogate's Court. It's the same court that will settle Louisa's estate. It's not that they consider Rufus to be her property, exactly. It's just how it's done.

"Ollie, I didn't tell you I went through the little packet of papers you gave me after Louisa's death. It's mostly the usual personal mementos—diplomas, report cards, a few love letters and pictures, like that. But there's also a statement of her intentions—almost like a will but a little like a suicide note, too. I probably should have given it to you at the time, but I thought you had enough on your plate."

"I'm sure you did the right thing, Prissy," I said. "You always do. But why is this important now?"

"Because Louisa said she wanted to leave Rufus in your care if anything should happen to her. She also said she had no idea who Rufus's biological father was, that he could have been one of several men. That his only role, whoever he may be, was enabling conception. And that he had never participated in Rufus's life, nor would she wish him to."

"Jesus, Prissy," I said. "Strong stuff."

"I've already introduced it in evidence. The court is considering it as they rule on Louisa's estate," she said. "And I think it should help your case."

"What can we expect, in court?" I asked.

"I'll look over everything again and text you anything that stands out. I expect the judge will ask if you're prepared to care for Rufus, personally and financially.   Your financials will be in evidence already. Mostly you'll have to declare your willingness to accept the responsibility of rearing a child. Courts in New York usually look favorably on single parents and gay parents, when other factors are strong. I'm not expecting any problems. It should be even easier for Rufus. The judge will probably ask him if he wants to have you as his parent. Once he's said yes, that should be it for him. You may be able to get him back to school after lunch. The case looks simple enough."

"Thanks, Prissy!" I said. "I'm looking forward to seeing you next week. And since I have you on the phone, I have some news for you."

"Oh? Do tell."

"Rick and I are getting married, in June," I said.

"Ollie, that's wonderful news!" she said. "But I'm not a bit surprised. I took one look at Rick at your dinner party and said to myself, 'Not only is he gorgeous, but he's obviously prime husband material. Can Ollie figure that out?' "

"Am I really that dense?" I asked.

"Yes, sometimes, but loveable always. Ollie, did you know I'm licensed to officiate at ceremonies? I'd love to perform yours."

"That's perfect, Prissy!" I said. "I hadn't thought of that. I guess I just hadn't gotten that far. Maybe Babby will stand up for us."

"Ask her," Priscilla said. "She loves a good wedding."

"Yes, I will," I said. "Please text me the details for next week, and Rufus and I will show up and perform on cue. And then, after that, we'll have to talk about new wills and all sorts of stuff. Anyway, thanks, Prissy! Talk soon." I was relieved, of course, that the legal fog might be lifting. Progress, yes. I went back to my desk and wrote a new chapter.

I know I said I wasn't worried about our future, but I still felt uneasy about Rick's career. So I was much cheered when he told me he had gone to Natural History, to the HR department, and scheduled an interview. His credentials were solid, and there had been a sort of cultural exchange for years between New York and DC. It looked promising. I thought we should celebrate—life, if nothing more. Rick agreed.

The three of us headed to Greenpoint that evening for Polish food. Neither Rufus nor Rick had ever tasted the condiment my favorite Greenpoint Polish places on the table with bread and pickles, after the dinner orders are in. Instead of butter, they offer a sort of *rillettes* that is as much lard as shredded pig. It's entirely too rich, and yet my men took to it as readily as I had embraced it a few years before.

We ate too many pierogis, and also kielbasa, sauerkraut, stuffed cabbage, and everything else they put in front of us. Over coffee, I asked Rufus, "So, how's school, little man? You haven't said a word about it in at least a week."

"It's fine, Uncle Ollie," he said.

"I'm not buying that," I said. "What's really happening?"

"Well, there's this kid who keeps messing with me."

"I think I know the one," Rick said. "Big kid. Named Schuyler." Rufus was silent.

"Look, Rufie, just tell him to stop fucking with you or you'll knock his head off," I said.

Rick said, "Ollie, that might work, but let me see what I can do first. Rufus, give me a few days." Rufus agreed. We took a taxi back to Manhattan. It dropped Rufus and me at home and took Rick on to his place. I hated having to say good night to Rick when he wouldn't be sleeping in my bed, but I was still grateful for our time together.

A few days later, Rick and I were having dinner while Rufus was at his Uncle Jerry's for one of his famous spaghetti nights. Rick said, "I may have made some progress with the school bully."

"What did you do?" I asked.

"I called Schuyler into my office. I sat him down, and I asked, 'Would you like to talk?'

" 'About what, sir?'

" 'About your behavior,' I said.

" 'What behavior?'

" 'I've seen you bully other children, Schuyler. There's no room for that in this school, nor indeed anywhere else in the world.' I waited. I wasn't certain where we were headed. He was silent for a bit. 'I'd like to help,' I said. 'I think you'd find me a good listener. And I know I can find the right *professional* listener to help you sort things out.'

"He said, 'I don't know, Mr. Kashani. That's not how we do things in my family.'

" 'Well, Schuyler, let me be blunt: If you continue in the direction you're headed, then never mind that you're about to flunk Science. I think your future at this school is in jeopardy.'

" 'What about *your* future at this school, sir?'

" 'Something else entirely,' I said. 'Let's focus on *yours*. I doubt you want to be expelled. I doubt you want your parents to be told that you are a sociopath. Are you listening to me, Schuyler?'

" 'Yes, sir.'

" 'It's entirely up to you,' I said. 'We could come to a gentlemen's agreement: my help and my silence in exchange for your civilized behavior. What do you think, Schuyler?'

" 'Yes, Mr. Kashani,' he said. We shook hands on it.

"I said, 'Feel free to come and talk to me any time, Schuyler.'

" 'Thanks, Mr. Kashani,' he said, and he left my office. I can't be certain how effective our agreement might prove, but it seemed like a start. I worry about troubled kids. If Schuyler asks for help, I'll get him to the right therapist. I'll do my best. But if I can just keep him from menacing other kids, then that's something, anyway. I hope."

"Rick, you're amazing," I said. "I couldn't begin to know how to do things like that."

"Don't be silly, Ollie." Rick said. "I've watched you with Rufus. I've seen you respond to his every issue and his every need. You have perfect instincts. Trust them."

"The only thing perfect in my life is my fiancé. Rick, I've known for a while now that you're the right man to help me—with parenting Rufus. I couldn't ask. I wouldn't. Except that he loves you already. So, will you? Help me?"

"Oliver, the words that come out of your mouth sometimes," Rick said. "You know I want us to be a family. And like all families, we'll sort out the particulars as we go along. Could we just enjoy being in love, for now? I think it's enough."

"It's better than that," I said. I gave Rick my hand, which he took, and I led him to my bed. There wouldn't be much time, before I needed to collect Rufus from Jerry's and get him home. There's never enough time for lovemaking, but Rick and I made the most of what time we had.

Chapter Sixteen

I thought I knew a lot about my parents. I had lived with them for fifteen years, after all. I was thinking about them because the concept of family was front and center in my brain and because I knew I'd have to tell Scarsdale about the wedding. I dreaded it, but it was necessary. I decided to try for something civilized. I phoned Cynthia and invited her to join me for lunch at '21'. She accepted. She must have questioned my motives, but she had few opportunities, these days, I assumed, to put on a hat and come into the city for lunch. And so she did.

"How is the child?" she asked as the hostess seated us.

"Rufus is doing great," I said. I had to do some fast thinking. "We should plan something." I wasn't born a Westchester WASP for nothing. I can play the game. That was about as deep as I was prepared to go with that. There would be no treks to Scarsdale for Rufus and me, nor would there be much in the way of other contact. But there were things that needed to be said—and done. We chose our luncheon dishes, and I ordered some wine.

"Aunt Cynthia, tell me about my mother," I said. "I thought I knew her, but now I'm not so sure."

"Funny you should ask, Oliver," she said. "I was just thinking about her so strongly as I was dressing to come here. We were very close when we were girls. By the time you met our parents—when you were a little boy—they had mellowed considerably. They probably seemed rather jolly when you saw them at holiday time, with a few toddies in them. Growing up with them was not so pleasant. Jenny was very protective of me. She had a wonderful way of diffusing the hurtful words that came out of Mother's mouth. I don't think I'd have survived it without her."

Shit! I thought. *What am I going to do with this can of worms, now that I've opened it?* "I didn't know," I said. "Mother always made everything seem nice. And safe."

"That was her way," Cynthia said. "When she married your father—he was so handsome, Oliver. It's really uncanny how much you resemble him. When she married, she naturally had new responsibilities. It's not exactly that we drifted apart. But it was different. She disliked Charles, so that created a bit of distance." I had no idea where to go with that. We completed our polite luncheon dishes. The waiter cleared. Cynthia asked for tea. I ordered coffee, and a shot to go in it. *Corretto*, Italians call it. That's my kind of correction.

"Aunt Cynthia," I began—I had to do it—"I'm to be married in June. I hope you'll come to the wedding."

"Well, Oliver," she said. "You know I've never approved of your lifestyle. But then, it really has nothing to do with me, does it?"

"You'll attend the wedding?" I asked. "I'd like you to be there. We don't have much family."

"I'll speak to Charles," she said. I took that as a tentative yes. As we were parting, I kissed Cynthia—

chastely on one cheek, of course—and handed her to her driver, who delivered her into the comfort of the back seat and sped her home, no doubt. I was uncertain about the jumble of feelings bouncing around in my body. I decided it didn't really matter whether I was feeling relief or anger or fear or resentment or even love. I had stated my case. It was time to turn its resolution over to the Universe.

Chapter Seventeen

I'd rather drink paint than have to go to court.
Maybe it's something to do with the custody hearings
after Mother and Dad died. It doesn't matter where
my legal phobia began, but it was very much on the
surface as we dressed to head downtown. Rufus
could still fit, just barely, into Sam's old suit. I
wanted Rufie to look properly cared for. He did. I
only hoped I could manage to look as respectable as
he did.

I ordered an Uber. We were quiet on the trip. Had
Jerry been with us, the atmosphere in the back seat
of that black SUV would have been considerably
brighter. But it was just Rufie and me. I put my
hand on his knee. He put *his* hand on *my* knee. We
smiled at each other. "What do you think, little
man?" I asked. "Does your old uncle have what it
takes to pull this off?"

"I don't know about my *old* uncle, but my *young*
uncle can do anything."

"Jesus, Rufe!" I said. "I do love you. Let's get this
done." I put my arm around him. We completed the
trip in silence. We both knew there was a lot riding
on the hearing we were about to attend. Priscilla
greeted us outside the courtroom. And to my surprise, Babby was with her.

Bruce K Beck

"I didn't want Rufus to be alone when you have to speak to the judge or whatever," Babby said. "Why don't you go with Prissy so she can update you, while I take Rufus over there. We can sit in the window. I brought him some hibiscus tea that's entirely too sweet. We're old friends." Rufus beamed.

"Thanks, Babby," I said. Everything started to look a little brighter. Priscilla took me aside and told me not to worry, that everything was in order, just as she had explained it to me the week before. She also told me our judge was famously tough but fair. I was feeling a bit numb. Babby and Rufus joined us, and we were all seated in the courtroom. Rufus and I were sworn in.

We rose to our feet for the entrance of the judge, the Honorable Frances Levy, who looked very stern indeed. She made me think of the nuns my Catholic friends told me about—the schoolteachers who rapped them on the knuckles with a ruler when they stepped out of line. I was pretty much in a state of terror. After the opening formalities, the judge said to me, "Mr. Hartmann, I've read your petition. I'd like you to explain what brings us here today—how we've gotten to this point."

"Yes, Your Honor," I said, and I took a deep breath. "Rufus and his mother—my sister Louisa— came to live with me in October, the month before her death. Since then I've been caring for Rufus. He started school in January. I walk him to school every morning and pick him up in the afternoons. We go to the gym three times a week. We share meals. I've done my best to create a normal life for him." I didn't know what else I could say, so I just stopped.

"Mr. Hartmann," the judge said, "you have provisional custody of the boy, I see. And it's your wish to change that to a parental role?"

"Yes, Your Honor."

"Are you aware of the responsibilities that accompany parenting?"

"Yes, Your Honor."

"It is *my* responsibility to the State of New York to place children in safe, loving families where their needs will be met. Do you feel you have that kind of home to offer your nephew?"

"I do, Your Honor," I said. "That's been my major focus since November." I didn't know what else I could say. I didn't know if I should profess my love for Rufus, for fear that might sound pervy. So I shut my mouth.

"Thank you, Mr. Hartmann," the judge said. I could have looked to Priscilla for feedback on my performance, but I didn't dare. I sat. I waited stonily. Next the judge said, "Mr. Hartmann . . ." This time she was addressing Rufus. The judge smiled at him rather sweetly and asked, "May I call you Rufus?"

"Yes, Your Honor." Prissy had obviously coached him well.

"Rufus, we've heard your uncle explain his understanding of the situation. Is that your understanding, too?"

"Yes, Your Honor."

"Is there anything you wish to add?"

"No, Your Honor," he said. "I think Uncle Ollie got it right." What a star!

"Rufus, your uncle said he wants to offer you a safe and loving home. How do you feel about that?"

"I feel like we've been a family ever since Mom died," Rufus said. "I wouldn't want it any other way." Definitely a star!

"Thank you, Rufus," the judge said. I looked at him and beamed. Judge Levy said, "We could take a brief recess while I consider my judgment, but I don't feel it's necessary. I'm satisfied we have all the information needed." I froze. "The court prefers to place children with their biological parents," she said. My icy feeling deepened. "In this case, there doesn't appear to be one." I warmed slightly. "A blood relative is often the next best option. The court is satisfied that everything is being done in the best interests of the child. Petition granted."

I grabbed Rufus and hugged him too hard. Then I embraced Priscilla, and then Babby. And I thanked the judge, who actually smiled at me. And then I floated out of the courtroom. "Shit, Rufe!" I said. "That nice judge says I'm your father, now! It's your fault, you know. You told her it was what you wanted. But you can always change your mind. You can just ask Ms. Lawson to reopen the case."

"I don't know, Uncle Ollie," he said. "That sounds like a lot of trouble. Let's just deal with what we have."

"Smart man," I said. "Are you hungry?"

"Very."

"In that case, I think we should get some lunch." I texted Rick the news. I knew I wouldn't be able to speak to him for hours. But I wanted him to know. Rufus and I thanked the ladies and said our good-byes. We walked uptown a few blocks to a Chinese noodle parlor. I said to the waiter, "My son is very hungry. Can you make him a soup with beef and chicken? And some vegetables? And maybe a shrimp or two?" The waiter agreed. I ordered the same, and then I began to think about what I had just said. "Rufe, how did that sound to you when I said 'my son'?"

"It sounded good."

"Are you sure that's what you want?" I asked.

"Uncle Ollie," he said. "Please stop asking me questions like that. Unless you changed your mind about me."

"Never, little man!" I said. "I was thinking maybe you've earned the rest of the day off from school. I made no promises about when I'd return you. I think we should do whatever we want to do today. What do you think?"

"I think you're having one of your good ideas, Uncle Ollie. Can we go to the zoo, in Central Park?

"You bet, Rufie," I said. The soup was good. It's easy to find a spicy condiment in Chinatown restaurants these days—a hot oil or sriracha—what with all the Southeast Asians and chili-hungry round-eyes in the clientele. I think a touch of chili oil wakes up a noodle soup beautifully. Rufus was a little tentative, but he gave it a try. He liked it too, once he had adjusted to the shock.

As we walked to the 6 train station, Rufus asked me, "What am I going to call you now?"

"I think you should call me whatever you like—within reason," I said. "I don't think our relationship is about forms of address. I think it's about our family and how we feel about each other."

"I think you're right, Uncle Ollie," he said. "I'm going to work on it."

"Take your time, little man," I said. "Meanwhile, the grizzly bears are waiting for you." I had fond memories from my childhood of the polar bears.

They're dead now, sadly. I remember reading both of their obits in *The New York Times*. The grizzlies were standing in nicely, however. Rufus and I had a delightful afternoon—relaxed and pressure-free. We ate ice cream. We walked home slowly. We got out of our courtroom drag and took well-earned naps.

Rick came to the apartment, late in the afternoon. He was nearly as excited about our news as I was. He brought us gifts—a beautiful pen for me and a journal for Rufus. We decided to go out for dinner. "I'm thrilled for you, Ollie!" Rick said. "Tell me about the hearing."

"I'm not sure I remember most of it, I was so nervous," I said. "But I certainly remember what a star Rufus was. When the judge spoke to him, he was cool as a cucumber, and he said all the right things. How did you learn to be so cool, little man?"

"From my Uncle Ollie. I learned everything I know from him."

"No, I think you learned *that* from your Uncle Jerry, but never mind. Let's order some food." And that's what we did. We ate. I drank more wine than I probably should have. And then we strolled home. Rufus ran ahead of us, to take the elevator upstairs. Rick and I spoke for a minute in the lobby before he headed to his place. I said to him, "Rick, I'm not making much sense, I know, but I just have to tell you how much I love you."

Rick said, "Ollie, could I just tell you how I feel today?"

"Of course, darling," I said.

"I feel that every day we get closer to the future we want to share. And today was a quantum leap. Sleep well, my love. I'll phone you tomorrow." He embraced me and offered a chaste kiss. And then he was off. I headed upstairs. When I let myself in, Rufus had already changed into his pajamas.

He said to me, "Could we watch a movie?"

"Sure," I said. "But it has to be something good. I don't want to spoil our day by ending it with trash. How about *NOW, YOYAGER*?"

"Whatever you think, Uncle Ollie," he said. "You know I like all the movies you like."

"Uh-huh, sure, I'm buying that," I said. "Rufie, do you have any idea how happy I am today?"

"I think so," he said. "You need to change your clothes. I'll boot the system in the living room." I changed into a robe and went to join Rufus. As I was setting up the picture, he asked me, "Did I ever tell you what Mom said about you?"

"I'm not sure. Try me," I said.

"She said, 'Your Uncle Ollie is a good man. You can trust him. We all need to know who we can trust. Ollie is solid. He won't let you down. Don't forget that.' "

"Your mother was so precious," I said. "I wish she could be with you always. She *is* with you always. You know that. You feel it, I'm sure you do, Rufus. But I wish she could have had dinner with us tonight. And I wish she could see how strong and brave you are. And handsome. You're going to be a knockout, buddy. You already are. You're going to break more hearts than Casanova. But even heartbreakers need to understand cinema. I'm about to show you the finest screen performance in the history of pictures." And I did.

Chapter Eighteen

The next afternoon, when I went to school to collect Rufus, I was greeted by an attractive woman about my age. I had seen her at school events, but we had never actually met. "Hello, I'm Joan McNamara, Charley's mother."

"Of course," I said. "I'm Oliver Hartmann, Rufus's father." I liked the sound of it.

"Yes, I know," she said. "I'm glad we're finally meeting." Joan smiled warmly. "I'm wondering if you'll let Rufus come over some afternoon, for a play date. He and Charley seem to be new best friends."

"Oh, thanks, Joan. That sounds great. But could we make it my apartment instead? I'm still not comfortable with Rufus out of my sight." I didn't tell her I worried that Rufus's maybe-biological-father might resurface. I decided that was too much information.

"Sure, Oliver," she said. "If you take both of the boys home with you some afternoon, then I can come for Charley about 5:00."

"Perfect," I said. We exchanged phone numbers, and I gave Joan my address. "How about tomorrow?" I asked.

"Yes, let's make it tomorrow. Charley's a good kid. I don't think you'll mind having him around."

"I'm certain I won't," I said. "Joan, what a pleasure. *I'm* glad we finally met, too." The boys appeared in the school doorway and joined us. Joan and I proposed the get-together. The boys were eager. We parted. As I walked Rufus home, I thought, *My son has a new friend! A schoolmate. A rich kid, probably. It can't hurt to know rich people. Rufus is on his way to normalcy!*

The next day, Betina was in to clean. She also made some *empanadas*. Rufus loved the ones filled with meat. And Betina seemed to enjoy making them for him. In fact, over the past few months, she had become quite motherly toward him. I was delighted to see I wasn't the only one who found him loveable. He could also charm a hard-working young Argentine woman who was far away from home and family.

I walked into the kitchen to refill my coffee cup as Betina was preparing the filling—she chopped hard-boiled eggs and green olives to add to the ground beef, along with other flavorings and enrichments. Betina said to me, "Mr. Hartmann, I have something to show you." I waited patiently while she wiped her hands and composed her thoughts. "When I was cleaning his room today, I found these." She opened a kitchen drawer and produced two girlie magazines! "I thought you should know."

"Betina, our little boy is growing up," I said. I had hoped that was all a few years away—the need to explore and understand our bodies, and all those hours spent in the bathroom masturbating. My own puberty was not so long past that I didn't remember it in detail. Rufus was not there, yet. He could still be a child for a while longer. But why shouldn't he be an informed child?

"Thanks for letting me know," I said. "I'm not worried about him. I was just trying to remember at what age I started looking at nudie magazines." I didn't mention that *my* nudes were male. Too much information. "Betina, would you put these back where you found them? I don't want Rufus to think we're checking up on him. He needs privacy as much as the rest of us do."

"Sure, Mr. Hartmann," she said. "I'll put them back. Mr. Hartmann, you're a nice guy."

"Thanks, Betina," I said. "Thanks for everything you do."

I met the boys at school that afternoon and walked them back to the apartment. They disappeared into Rufus's very red and black room, only surfacing to dash to the kitchen for Betina's freshly fried *empanadas*. I was having a good time, too. I liked the simplicity of it; the ordinariness of it; the normality of it. Yes, the play date was going well.

Joan arrived shortly after 5:00 to collect Charley. "I said to her, "I've just opened a bottle of wine. Will you have a glass, if you're not in a rush?"

"Thanks, Oliver," she said. "That's kind of you. Yes, I'll stay for a bit. My housekeeper is making dinner tonight, so I don't have to dash." I poured. We took our glasses to the living room. We sat. Joan flashed me that winning smile of hers. She complimented the wine and asked me the name of it. I studied her, briefly, and determined that my first impression was spot-on: She was a very handsome woman, indeed—fair, sporty, at ease in her skin. Privilege has its rewards.

"I love this apartment, Oliver," she said. "Have you been here long?"

"Since right after college," I said. "So, I won't confess how long ago that was. I've been very happy here."

"It shows," she said. "And I sense you're making a fine home for Rufus, too."

"Thanks, Joan. That's a kind thing to say. It's my goal."

"Oliver, there's something I have to tell you." Joan grew quiet, and everything about her seemed to darken. I waited. "I'm not proud of it, but I spoke to the Headmaster about you and Mr. Kashani."

"But why, Joan? Why would you do that?" I asked.

"If I'm going to be honest, I'll have to say it was jealousy."

"But Joan," I said, "what could you possibly be jealous of?"

"I saw you and Mr. Kashani at a school event, and it was obvious to me that the two of you were very much in love. I haven't felt the thrill of young love in a lot of years. There, I've said it out loud." We were silent for a bit. We sipped our wine. I waited for more information. "I spoke to my husband about it. He suggested that I mind my own fucking business, pardon my French. But I couldn't quite let go of it. I thought you deserved to know," she said. "I won't ask for your forgiveness, or Mr. Kashani's."

"Jesus, Joan!" I said. "I thought I was just hosting a play date today. You've given me a lot to process. I don't know. I can't speak for Rick, but neither of us is much into recrimination. I think we should probably just let go of this. But why don't we speak again, the next time the boys come here to play?"

"That's very generous of you, Oliver," she said.

"I won't tell Rick about it." I said. "I think that's up to you. I mean, I think it's your responsibility to tell him."

"Yes, of course," she said.

"It occurred to me, Joan," I said, "that I probably didn't tell you that Rick and I are getting married in mid-June. Will you come?"

"Yes, Oliver," she said. "I'd love to. And I know Charley and his father will want to be there, too."

"Good," I said. "And I think that's enough drama for one day." The boys came bounding out of Rufus's room, and Charley and his mother gathered their things to leave. I gave Joan a chaste kiss on one cheek as they were heading out the door. She smiled sweetly, and they were gone. Really, what can we do with people? Don't we just have to practice forgiveness and love, even when it hurts?

"Betina, Rufus and I were supposed to make dinner tonight," I said. "If your wonderful *empanadas* haven't already spoiled his appetite, then I think we should go out. Will you join us? What do you say to Cuban Chinese?"

"I'm not sure I know what that is, Mr. Hartmann," Betina said. "But yes. I'll try anything once." *Good answer*, I thought. And that's what we did.

Will phoned me the next week. "Will you have dinner with me? Maybe on Friday? Like we used to do?"

"Sure," I said. What else could I say? I was nervous about seeing Will again. I spoke to Rick about it.

"Ollie," Rick said, "you haven't seen Will in months. People don't stop loving people just because they're apart. You deserve a chance to see him again. Don't make yourself crazy about this. It's dinner."

"That's what I told myself before my first date with Will," I said. "And then dinner turned into—never mind. Rick, your love makes me so happy! I don't need to step back into my past."

"Thanks, Ollie, for that," Rick said. "But I'm certain the man I love will have dinner with *one* of his loves and find something important to take away from it. If it's closure, then great. If it's yearning, then you'll tell me, and we'll deal with it. Ollie, you don't really think you can duck this, do you?"

"Jesus, Rick!" I said. "Are there Persian saints? Because you seem to be a candidate." And my sainted fiancé even offered to babysit Rufus on Friday night. My cup was beyond running over—it was spilling everywhere.

<h2>Chapter Nineteen</h2>

"How long has it been since one of our Friday dinners?" Will asked. "Never mind," he said. "Ollie, it's wonderful to see you."

"Yes, Will," I said. "I've missed you, too." We met at the French restaurant that's been there for so many years, the one in the big corner building on Amsterdam all covered in terra-cotta. The restaurant was as welcoming as ever. Will was as handsome as ever. Maybe more so. We were seated. We ordered. Will chose the wine.

"You look great . . ." we both started to say, in unison. Then we stopped, smiled, and retreated from the automatic niceties. "Ollie, I've wanted to phone you so many times," Will said. "But we agreed."

"Yes," I said. "And so, why now?" Why, indeed?

"Yes, Ollie," he said. "Thank you for getting to the point. Could we enjoy the soup before I have to start baring my breast?"

"I always preferred your breast bare, but I'll allow you some cover, if you need it. Good soup. I always did like cucumber/gazpacho-like things." We finished it. The waiter cleared. "Will, you know what's coming next: the duck that already bared its breast. So, when will it be your turn?"

"Ollie, will you wait until after the duck—for me to strip? I can do it over coffee, I think. I'm not sure I'll be ready until then."

"Jesus, Will," I said. "I feel like we're sparring. That doesn't make any sense for two people who love each other. I don't want to challenge you. I just want to enjoy an evening with you. Please forgive me for coming on strong. I think you have something to tell me, and I think you should tell me whenever you fucking well please, and not a moment sooner."

"Ollie, you take my breath away," Will said. "But then you always did." We finished our duck in silence. Will ordered a dessert for us to share. My heart wasn't in it, but I tried to be a good sport. Polite bites of chocolate and caramelized pear. And then, of course, over coffee, it was time for Will to get naked. "Ollie, I told you about Jennifer," he said. "I talked to Sam about it, of course. He seemed pleased about the idea of our getting back together. But he seemed reserved. He seemed to be waiting for *my* reaction. I let it go for nearly a week."

I flagged down the waiter and ordered a *framboise*. Will declined. I felt the need of a little sweet blindness. I had no idea where Will's story was going, but I sensed that whatever turn it might take, it had nothing good to offer me. I smiled. I sipped my coffee. I sipped my *eau de vie*. I waited.

"Then I phoned Jennifer," Will said. "She suggested that Sam and I go to Boston to stay with her. As a sort of test. I knew Sam would be happy to go. I agreed, on the condition that I would stay in a hotel. It was all arranged—for two weeks later. The days that followed my decision were some of my bleakest. I had no faith in my judgment. The trip assumed a life of its own, while I was merely along for the ride."

Will paused for a sip of coffee, and to gather his thoughts. Then he resumed. "Sam was glad to see his mother, of course. He had gone to Boston at least twice a year for the previous five years, while I had studiously avoided that city entirely. Sam was pleased. Jennifer was pleased. I was miserable. Seeing her again seemed to rip the scab from my heart, leaving a fresh wound. Jennifer is a beautiful woman. The years have only enhanced her beauty. I knew exactly why I fell in love with her more than a decade before. I could go back there. I was sure I could. I was equally sure that I most certainly did not want to.

"Sam stayed with his mother, as we had agreed. I joined them for meals and outings. It was all very civilized. I could almost believe that we could re-group our little family. Almost. Then, on the morning of the third day, Sam joined me for break-fast at my hotel. I asked him, 'What do you think, Sammy? Is this what you want? For your mother and me to get back together?'

"Well, Ollie, you understand. You have a child. You know how smart they are. Sam said to me, 'Dad, I'd love for us to be a family again. But I see you and Mom together. And I see how unhappy it makes you. I think you and I should go home. We've managed without her so far. I think we'll be fine.' I grabbed him and hugged him a little too hard. 'Dad, I can't breathe,' he said.

" 'I love you, Sammy,' I said. 'Let's go home.' And that's what we did. I packed my bag, and we headed to Jennifer's so Sam could pack his. I gave her my decision while Sam was packing. Jennifer was dis-appointed but not shocked, I think. We didn't drag it out. Both of us had lost all taste for drama, I think.

Sam kissed her goodbye. *I* kissed her goodbye. And Sam and I were on the afternoon train."

"Will," I said, "it sounds like you did just the right thing."

"Thanks for that, Ollie," he said. "I hope you're right."

"How is Sam taking it?" I asked. "Kids are so resilient. I'll bet he's just fine."

"Yes, I think so," Will said. "Ollie, there's something else I want to tell you." I was glad for the fortification in my glass. It minimized the sinking feeling that came over me. I knew there was something else. I had known it all evening. Maybe since Will phoned me. I just had no idea what it was.

"There's a new apartment building going up in the neighborhood—where isn't there one? This building is beautifully designed, actually, and now, before it's finished, I could take two units and reconfigure them into the perfect space for the four of us. With great views, too! What do you think, Ollie?"

"I think I'm speechless, Will," I said. "Let me catch my breath." I didn't hyperventilate, but nearly. Will looked so pleased. The previous winter, I would have been even more excited than he was. But then, of course, everything had changed. "I always said we needed the Housing Fairy to wave the wand and combine our households. I just never dreamed the Housing Fairy would be you.

"Will, I can't begin to tell you how honored I feel, that you would rearrange your life for me. But *my* life is already rearranged, since the last time we spoke. Will, I have to just say it: I'm getting married in a few weeks. I hope you and Sam will come to the wedding. I want you there, and I'm sure Rufus will, too. It's not nice of me to spring it on you like that. But we haven't spoken in months."

"I'm going to be very happy for you, Ollie, as soon as I get over my shock," Will said. "I'm sure he's a wonderful man. It is a man you're marrying, yes?"

"Yes, Will," I said. "You're the fluid one. Not me. You'll love Rick when you get to know him. He's a fine man."

"He'd have to be, if you love him. Ollie, I'm so pleased for you. You deserve to find the one who completes your life. Could I ask one question?"

"Of course, Will."

"If I had been available, last winter, would you have committed to me?"

"Yes, Will. You know that," I said.

"I felt that was the truth of it, but I had to ask. I'll always remember that you loved me, and that I got it wrong."

"Jesus, Will," I said, "please don't say that. I *still* love you. Always will. And nobody got anything wrong. It just is what it is."

"We seem to be saying goodbye at our every meeting," Will said. "Ollie, I want to thank you for walking into my life, for catching the ball, for letting me love you, and for awakening something in me that I thought was long buried." I was quiet. I've never had much stomach for endings. And this one? As painful as any.

We said our good nights on the sidewalk in front of the restaurant. Will kissed me. I kissed him back. We both knew it was our last, most likely. We made the most of it. We parted. I headed home with a heavy heart. But the closer I got to my building—to Rufus and to the new life Rick and I would build there—the more I knew that everything was just as it should be.

When I let myself in, Rufus had gone to bed, and Rick was napping in front of the TV with a book open on his beautiful chest. I sat down next to him, and he awakened. "Was it CNN or the book that put you to sleep?" I asked.

"Maybe both," he said. "How was dinner?"

"It was fine," I said. "I've always liked the food there."

"That's not what I meant, of course," Rick said.

"I know, darling," I said. "Can I tell you about it tomorrow?"

"Of course," he said. "I think we should get some sleep. We have a big day tomorrow. Rufus is so excited about the penguin house at the Bronx Zoo. I loved it too, when I was his age and my parents brought me to New York." I kissed Rick. Deeply. He said, "That was delicious, but I also taste another man. It's good, but I'd prefer just tasting you. What do you think?"

"I think you're perfect, and I think you'll be tasting only me for as long as you'll have me."

"Wise answer," Rick said. "Come to bed, darling." I managed to get my teeth brushed, but not much else before I dove into my bed and into Rick's embrace. He said something completely unintelligible to me that I assumed was "Sleep well, my love," in Farsi. I wrapped myself around Rick and drifted into blissful sleep.

Chapter Twenty

On Tuesday morning, as we left my building as usual, I began to feel vaguely uneasy—as if we were being followed. My eyes darted all around, but I couldn't see anything or anyone unusual. I put my hand on Rufus's shoulder and drew him close as I picked up my pace. I felt a bit foolish about my uneasiness, but then I've learned, through the years, that my instincts are generally worth honoring. When we reached the school, I reminded Rufus that Betina would pick him up at 3:00 because I had an appointment with a publisher. He gave me the familiar eye roll. I said, "I love you, Rufie." He flashed me his best grin and headed into the building.

As I walked away, I noticed a man who seemed out of place. It wasn't because he was a gorgeous black man, it was because he didn't look like a parent. He was simply standing there, in front of the school, rather than saying goodbye to a child and scurrying off to work or home as the rest of us did. He noticed me, as well. He headed toward me. I would have preferred not to make eye contact, but there didn't seem to be any way to avoid it.

"Aaron Mosely," he said as he extended his hand.

"Oliver Hartmann," I said as I shook it, reluctantly.

"I know who you are," Aaron said. "I'm Rufus's father. We need to talk." Was I shocked? Not really. I had expected him to surface. I'd thought often about how I would handle this inevitability. And yet I felt ill prepared.

"There's a Starbucks about two blocks that way," I said. I figured a very public place would be the safest way to stage our meeting. Aaron agreed. We walked in silence. We got in line. We placed our orders. Separately. We waited for our coffees, and then we found a small table. I studied the beauty across from me. No wonder Louisa fell for him. But I reminded myself that he was abusive to her, and that he probably introduced her to heroin—an overdose of which was declared the official cause of her death. I asked, "What are you doing here, Aaron?"

"Well, Oliver, I want to thank you for looking after Rufus. I was out of town when Louisa died. I didn't even hear about it until February. But I'm back now."

"And?"

"And I want to take him home with me."

"Why?" I asked.

"Because he's my son, and he should be with his father."

"That's not what Louisa said."

"What?" he asked.

"Louisa said whoever fathered Rufus—any one of several men—was merely a sperm donor. That's what she said. What do you say?"

"Oliver, your sister and I loved each other very much, and we created a child from that love. I'm trying to do the right thing by him."

"Aaron, what do you really want? I'm not buying the fatherhood angle."

"You're a cold man, Oliver. Maybe you've never been in love."

"I'll let that pass," I said. "Let's talk about Rufus. What do you have to offer him?"

"I have a place," he said. "I have a lady, now, who loves children. We want him to live with us."

"So, you're ready to pay for his school and his clothing and his food?" I asked. "Do you have the slightest idea what it costs to send a child to school?"

"I figured his mother's family would pay for that."

"And what else did you figure we'd pay for?" I asked.

"Look, Oliver, I don't know what you're trying to imply."

"I'm not trying to imply anything. I'm telling you, directly, that I don't believe you. And I don't see any reason to continue this conversation."

"Oliver, I know where you live, and I'm going to show up there tomorrow afternoon. And you'd better have Rufus packed and ready to go with me."

"Aaron, I hope you're listening to me," I said. "Rufus is my child. It's what his mother wanted. It's what the court wants. And there's nothing you can do to change that. If you make trouble, I swear I'll kill you if necessary. Yes, that's a threat."

Aaron began to laugh. "You talk big, for a faggot."

"This faggot is stronger than he looks. Test me, if you want. I'll rip your heart right out of your chest, if that's what it takes to stop you from interfering with his life. You will not cause Rufus any more pain. It's not going to happen. Do we understand each other? You're going to disappear from our lives. Now. And if you ever try this again, I'll make sure you're locked up and that they throw away the key."

Big talk, indeed. I was quaking with outrage—and terror, of course.

"Let's settle on . . ."

"Not one fucking penny," I said. "You think I'm a chump? You think I don't know you're looking to milk a cash cow? If I were you, Aaron, I'd get out of this Starbucks as quickly as possible. If I have to look at your very pretty face much longer, I'll be tempted to rearrange it. Another threat."

"Oliver, Rufus is coming with me. Have him ready tomorrow afternoon."

"Aaron, maybe you're forgetting I know you murdered my sister. And now you think I'll let you anywhere near her child? Well, think again. You don't look like an idiot, but you're certainly acting like one."

"Cut the shit, Oliver. Have him ready."

"We have excellent police presence on Central Park West. I'll head to the precinct right now to report you. I'm a writer. I'm good at giving descriptions. Let me see, do you mind if I take a quick video of you on my phone? That will help with ID." Aaron lunged for my phone. I was ready for him. I secured it in my pocket. "Well, it doesn't matter," I said. "You're on the surveillance camera footage in front of Rufus's school. I know exactly when you were there this morning, so I'm sure there will be no trouble finding your picture. There aren't many men as handsome as you are. Pity."

"Well, sissy boy. Maybe you won. This round. But I'll be back."

"I'll do everything I said to keep Rufus safe from you. But if you find a way to get anywhere near him, then they'll find what's left of you floating in the Hudson. And that's more than a threat. It's a promise."

There was steely silence between us. And then I had second thoughts: *I've just tried to cut this man off at the knees, and that's going to solve problems? That's going to ensure that we'll lose the threat of his return? I don't think so.*

"Could we back up a little, please?" I said. "Look, Aaron, I don't think you're a monster. You wouldn't get out of this room alive if I did. But I don't think you understand what's at stake here. You say you loved Louisa. Let's say I believe you. Then the only honorable thing to do is to step aside and let Rufus get on with his life. There's nothing here for you. I hope you can accept that and walk away."

I couldn't tell quite where the exchange was hovering. Aaron looked defiant, but thoughtful. We finished our coffee. I reached into my pocket and took out my key chain, where I had added a gold charm of Louisa's—a heart. I removed it and pressed it into Aaron's palm. I said, "Please take this and leave us in peace." Eventually, Aaron stood up, smiled, and left the Starbucks with considerable swagger. And not a moment too soon, as far as I was concerned. I had spent my quota of bluster for the decade, most likely.

I did go to the precinct to report Aaron, of course. I didn't get my video, but I did get a snapshot that was clear enough. I told the police exactly when he had been in front of the school, so they could find him on the surveillance video. And then I walked to school to report Aaron to security, so they would know never to release Rufus to him, under any circumstance.

When I got home, I told the doorman about him. I asked Jake to call the police if he ever saw Aaron anywhere near the building. "I understand, Mr.

Hartmann," Jake said. "I'll tell the other guys. Security is part of our job. We'll take care of it." I wondered what they might have in their security arsenal, behind the desk. A police-calling button? Jake held up a walkie-talkie. He said, "Direct to the precinct." A taser? A gun? Probably not, I thought. I didn't ask. I didn't want to know.

I rescheduled my 3:00 and went to school instead. Betina was surprised to see me, of course. I told her—and Rufus—it was a last-minute cancelation, and I suggested the three of us go out for a snack. They agreed. We had a good time, and then we parted. I walked Rufus home without a word to him about Aaron. I couldn't. I didn't want to upset him, and there didn't seem to be a real reason to raise any more alarms.

I decided I wouldn't tell Rufus about my meeting with the man who might be his father. I decided. I seemed to be deciding everything. What about Rufus? Did he deserve to know? "What am I doing?" I asked Rick. "This could be his last chance to see his biological father."

"Ollie, stop beating yourself up," Rick said. "Rufus doesn't have a biological father. He has you. And I think you'll do just fine. And so does he. Give it a rest." And that's what I did, mostly.

Chapter Twenty-one

Rufus's birthday fell on the last day of school that year. I thought about a party. But then I realized I'd be inviting mostly the same people who would be coming to the wedding in two weeks. It seemed like overkill. Instead, Rick volunteered to prepare a special dinner, and we asked Jerry to join us. It would be plenty festive.

I was uncertain how to gift Rufus. In the end, I decided to buy him a new dark suit—one that really fit him. That way he would be the best-dressed member of the wedding party. I took him to Saks the Saturday before his birthday. The salesclerk took a few measurements and brought out the perfect suit, exactly Rufus's size. One and done. A little finishing and we could pick it up the next week.

I also chose a few shirts and ties. Or rather, Rufus chose some ties. They were not the ones I'd have picked out for him—Rufus's choices were brighter and livelier than mine. Younger? Perhaps. And then we went to lunch to celebrate our shopping success. It was a fun time. When we got home, there was a package waiting for me. I took it with me to my room when I went to change. A quick glance at the return address told me it came from Aaron. I put the package on my desk and out of my mind. More or less. I got on with my afternoon.

If Rufus had asked me about the package, I'd have told him it was something from a publisher. Nothing unusual there. Rick would be arriving soon. I was dying to see him, as always. After Rick kissed me, he said, "Ollie, I forgot to tell you last night: The mother of one of my students asked me to stop by after school on Monday for a glass of wine. You know her, I think: Joan McNamara, Charley's mother. What could this be about?"

"I don't have to guess," I said. "I know. But I can't talk about it. It's up to her. I told her I wouldn't be an intermediary. Please trust me, darling. Please let her say what she needs to say."

"Aren't you the mysterious one," Rick said. "Very well. I'll wait until Monday."

"There's another mystery, as it turns out," I said. I went to my desk and picked up the package. I showed it to Rick. He seemed less shocked than I was.

"It's obviously a birthday gift for Rufus," Rick said. "See, that's what happens when you treat people like humans. Why don't you take it out of the shipping wrapper?"

"So smart," I said. "What a husband I'm getting!" I did unpack it. Rick was right, of course. It was a giftwrapped box with a card. "Rick, what am I going to do with this?"

"I don't see many choices, Ollie. Most likely you're going to give it to Rufus next week on his birthday. But maybe you should read the card, to make sure it's safe. That may not be entirely ethical, but I think it's necessary."

"Thanks, Rick." I said. "That's exactly what I'll do." The envelope wasn't sealed, fortunately. I slipped out the card and read it. It was signed:

For Rufus, with birthday wishes
from your mother's friend, Aaron Mosely

"Shit!" I said. "Darling, what have I done?"

"Shut up, Ollie," Rick said, as he gripped me. "You've done exactly what any good parent would do. You've protected your child."

"He'll figure this out, and he'll hate me. I know he will." Rick tightened his grip.

"Ollie, stop it!" he said. "Rufus loves you as much as I do. Whatever he guesses or surmises or wonders about, he will never question your motives. He couldn't. You showed him your heart. Just as you showed it to me."

"Thanks, Rick," I said. "I hope you're right. Anyway, enough of that. I have *days* before I need to freak-out about this fucking birthday gift. Meanwhile, what would you like for dinner?"

Rick came to the apartment on Monday evening, after his meeting with Joan. "That was strange," he said. "I guess I understand why you wouldn't talk about it."

"Even though her complaint to the Headmaster concerned both of us, I knew the only damage she did was to you. And I figured she had to man up and make her own apology."

"Well, that's what she did," Rick said. "I had a quick flash of anger, but I let go of it right away. And before long, I realized I quite like her. She told me you invited her to the wedding."

"Was that crazy?" I asked. "I can't say exactly what I was thinking, but it seemed like the right thing to do. We need all the allies we can get. I could have thrown her out, but really, what's the point in antagonizing straight people?"

"No point at all. I love you, Ollie. You have such a good heart. Don't change a thing." Rick kissed me, very sweetly. And then he said, "Speaking of Joan and career damage, I have a second job interview at Natural History on Wednesday, after school. I don't know, of course, but it feels like just a formality. The woman who phoned to schedule the appointment heads up the education department. I would be working for her, essentially. She seems quite solid and collegial. Her tone felt—welcoming, really. I may be just optimistic, but I think it looks good."

"Of course it does, my love," I said. "Could I get another kiss from my favorite natural historian?" I did get one, of course.

"This has all gone rather smoothly, I think," Rick said. "I'm so glad the old fart came through with a recommendation letter. Did I show it to you?"

"No, darling."

"Sorry. I have a copy in my office. It's glowing, actually."

"And why not?" I asked. "You're a wonderful teacher, and your morals are above reproach. If he knew what a fabulous lover you are, he'd have had even more good things to say about you. But I prefer to keep that to myself."

"Wise," Rick said. "Wise and hot. A fine combination. Do we have time before dinner to find out if it's true?"

"That you're a fabulous lover? There's always time to prove that. Come here, you!" And that's what we did.

Rufus was excited about his birthday—and the last day of school. Jerry phoned to ask if he could buy Rufus a puppy. I was skeptical. "Oh, Jer, I don't know," I said. "It sounds like a lot of work."

"It's a commitment, of course," Jerry said. "But I think it would be good for Rufus. And for you, too."

"Oh, Jerry, what can I say? Of course. Do it! As long as you're willing to board the doggie if we need to go away for some reason. Families do take vacations, you know."

"Of course, Ollie," he said. "I love dogs. I haven't owned one since I was a kid. But I'm willing."

"I love you, Jerry," I said. "Carry on." Rick came by after school with some groceries for the birthday dinner. I told him the news.

"Darling, that's perfect! I'm only sorry I didn't think of it myself," Rick said. "But you don't seem sold on the idea. Why, Ollie?"

"Why, indeed?" I said. "I've been trying to figure out why I'm uneasy about it. Rufus will love it. And you know he'll take responsibility. He's that kind of kid. And I think you'll be happy to help with late-night walks and such."

"Yes."

"So, this is something of mine, don't you think? All I can tell you is that when Mother and Dad died, Cynthia and Charles were willing to take Louisa and me in, but not our pets. I think they all went to a vet who put them down. That's what I think happened. More loss of loved ones. I've never considered creating a bond like that since. I don't think my heart could stand the loss of it."

"Your heart can stand anything, Ollie," Rick said. "If I die tomorrow, you'll get right up and love again. It's who you are. Never forget that." I embraced Rick. We were silent for a while. I had no words to accompany the warmth that surged through me. "Let me put the groceries away," he said. "I'll soak the *porcini*. And I'll start the sauce. Then all I have to do on Thursday is assemble the *lasagne* and get the pan in the oven."

On Thursday, when Jerry arrived with our new family member—in a tote bag lined with diapers—I thought Rufus would pop. A little French bulldog. Jerry said to me, "Frenchies are very popular, of course, but the breeder assured me they're perfect apartment dogs and totally kid-friendly. You'll forgive me for this, some day."

"I already have," I said. "Let me make you a drink."

Jerry said, "Rufus, what do you want to name him? It's up to you. He has a long pedigree, but you get to decide what to call him."

"My first thought was to call him Jerry, but that might be confusing," Rufus said.

"It's up to you, nephew," Jerry said. "I don't often have animals named after me, but as long as it isn't a pig or a tarantula, I don't mind the idea. But how about Jerome, then?"

"Yes," Rufus said. "He looks like Jerome. Welcome home, Jerome." And the puppy squirmed his way up Rufie's chest in an effort to get as close as possible. Yes. It was going well. Betina put some newspapers down on the kitchen floor. She was so practical. I was glad I thought to invite her to Rufus's party. We needed her at our family celebration as much as we needed anyone else. Betina brought a special dessert—something with coconut that would most likely be achingly sweet. Perfect.

After Jerome, other gifts would naturally be underwhelming. Rick and I had gotten Rufus a few little things. Mostly, though, I had to give him Aaron's package—as casually as possible. I blessed Jerome for the distraction. I handed the box to Rufus. He slipped the card out of the envelope and read it. "I remember him," Rufus said. He didn't look up at me, fortunately, because I couldn't seem to get my poker face on right. Rufus unwrapped the package. It was a chemistry set. He brightened. It was a perfect gift, actually. Rufus and Rick examined it, briefly, and planned the first experiments they would conduct together. And then it was time to go to the dining table.

Rick outdid himself that night. Dinner was delicious. I gave Rufus a wine glass with water and a splash of red, for the first time. He seemed to like it. Betina's dessert was just as sweet and just as perfect for a kid's birthday as I had assumed it would be. After coffee, Betina got up from the table and began to organize the kitchen and start the cleanup.

"Betina, you're a guest tonight," I said. "Leave that."

"But Mr. Hartmann, it will only take a few minutes," she said. As I was wrangling with her, Jerry came to say good night. He gave me the nutrition starter kit and instructions the breeder had sent along. I walked him to the door.

"Jerry, you're amazing," I said. "But then you always were." He kissed me, and he headed home. I returned to the kitchen. I said, "Thank you, Betina, but that's enough of that. When do we see you again, Monday?" I went and got her jacket. I held it for her as I said, "Okay, lady. Off you go." I called to Rufus to tell him she was leaving. He dashed into the kitchen.

"Thank you, Betina," he said. And he kissed her. She touched his face, and then she headed home. Rick joined us in the kitchen, carrying Jerome. I put my arms around Rick and the rest of my family. I only hoped Rufus had as good a day as I did.

"Do I need to write a thank-you card?" Rufus asked. "To Aaron."

"That's up to you, Rufie," I said. "Do you want to send him a card?"

"I don't know," he said. Rufus seemed to be processing history. I guessed he was remembering how Aaron made his mother cry. I thought I knew my child well enough to get a handle on the situation. And yet? What does any parent know about those complex creatures in our care?

"I don't know," Rufus said. "I'll talk to Jerome about it. Can he sleep with me?"

"Maybe *next to* you, tonight?" I suggested.

Rick said, "Rufie, there's a tub in the laundry room that's just about his size. Let's line it with the diapers Jerry brought and set it up next to your bed. I think Jerome will be very comfortable there."

As they headed off to get Rufus and Jerome settled in for the night, I rinsed some plates and finished loading the dishwasher. And I said to myself, "Oliver, you have the perfect child and the perfect mate, and now you have the perfect pet. Any more joy might prove fatal!"

Chapter Twenty-two

There was a heavy downpour on the morning of our wedding day. From my bedroom window I could see the park all dark and brooding. I turned on extra lights in my room to counter the gloom. By noon, when we'd all be arriving at the Gardens, there was the likelihood of clear skies and lots of sun. But then we all know how iffy forecasts can be. I wasn't concerned. There's a pavilion in the Gardens where we could stage the ceremony, if need be. I was more concerned about finding some decent cufflinks in my jewelry box. I thought I had Dad's: the gold ones with the black onyx. There were shirt studs in the set, surely. Four of them. And yet I couldn't seem to find any of it.

I called to Betina, who was already in the apartment, organizing the reception. She came to my room and said, quietly, "Mr. Hartmann, you don't keep gold there. You keep gold in the little safe under your bed."

"Quite right, Betina," I said. "Thank you. And thanks for taking care of us today. I always know I can relax when you're in charge." Betina smiled. It was good to see her smile. She didn't do it very often.

"No pay today, Mr. Hartmann," Betina said. "I'm here as a friend."

"That's entirely too generous, Betina," I said. "We'll talk about it later." I embraced her, for the first time, most likely. Weddings have that effect on people. "Thanks again." She returned to the kitchen. I returned to my hunt for the various parts of my wedding outfit. My door was open. Rufus bounded in—with Jerome in his arms, of course—and jumped up onto my bed.

"When is Rick coming?" he asked. My first thought was to correct Rufus—to remind him of his responsibility to address Rick as Mr. Kashani. But then I realized that was a vestige of the past. Our new life was beginning. And it was good.

"He should be leaving his apartment any minute. Is there anything you need—anything he can pick up on his way over?" We had decided Rick should sleep at his place the night before. It wasn't because of any superstition about couples not seeing each other before the wedding, but because it made sense for him to dress at home, rather than bringing things to my place and risking forgetting something.

"I'm good," Rufus said. "Can Jerome come to the wedding?"

"I don't know, Rufie," I said. "He's so small. I don't think it's a good idea. But let's talk to Rick about it when he gets here."

"Okay," Rufus said. "You seem nervous. Is everyone nervous on their wedding day?"

"I can't speak for everyone, Rufie," I said, "but your old uncle has a case of nerves, for sure. Would you bring me a glass of soda with a few dashes of bitters and a big splash of gin?"

"Sure, Daddy, but promise me you won't drink too much today."

I was dumbfounded. "Rufus, did you really call me Daddy? Or did I imagine that?"

"Sure," he said. "I like the sound of it. How about you?" I swept him up into my arms, leaving Jerome to fend for himself. Rufus was growing so fast that I doubted I'd be able to hold him that way too many more times. But that morning—the morning of my wedding day—Rufus was still my little boy. I held him as long as I dared. And then I put him down.

"Please get your dad that beverage," I said. "And then you and Betina should probably give Jerome a quick walk. We don't want him peeing on the floor during the reception. And then you should probably get dressed. Thanks, Rufie." I hadn't even gotten to the altar yet, and already I was weepy. It would be that kind of day, surely. Rick arrived a few minutes later. He had stopped at the florist's for our boutonnières and for wrist corsages for the ladies. We had already arranged flowers for the reception the night before.

"Rick, you are so beautiful, I can't think what I did to deserve you," I said.

"Imagine if we only got what we deserve," Rick said. "Let's take what we can get." I took the biggest kiss I could get. I had no desire for the Conservatory Gardens or friends or family. I just wanted Rick in my bed. But we had plans. Reservations were made and paid. It would be a lovely day, surely. Betina was finishing her preparations. Surely we had ordered enough cases of champagne. The first two were iced. The rest were in a cool place. Rufus was in his room getting dressed. Rick came with me to my room. I asked him to help me with the shirt studs. As he got me fastened into my overstarched shirt, Rick said, "Oliver, I have a request."

"What is it, darling?"

"I want a wedding gift."

"Anything. What can I give you?"

"I want a book with your name on it," Rick said. I teared up, for the second time that day—and surely not the last.

"You shall have it," I said. "Whatever my husband desires he shall have. I'll start it right after our honeymoon. How long will that be, by the way? I don't think we really planned it."

"You'd better start the book sooner than that, because I intend to honeymoon for decades," Rick said. I'd have grabbed him and wrapped myself around him like a python, except that we were both dandified for the upcoming ceremony. I settled for a kiss. We were ready. Betina was ready. Rufus was ready. What a star! He looked terrific in his new suit. As I pinned a flower on his lapel, I thought, *This kid looks so comfortable, but he looks just as comfortable in a T-shirt and jeans. He's comfortable in his skin. And, after all, what more could I wish for my son?*

"Rick, can Jerome come to the wedding?" Rufus asked. "Daddy said you'd know."

Rick shot me a quick look and then went right into his response. "Sorry, Rufie. He's too young. He needs time for his vaccinations to protect him. It's too early for him to be around a bunch of people and maybe wild animals in the park. We'll have other celebrations. Why don't you put him in his box, by your bed? He'll probably sleep through the whole thing."

Jerry hired an Uber—a big one—to drive the five of us to the Gardens. The storm system had cleared, as predicted. It was a perfect day for a garden wedding. Prissy and Babby were already there, and they both looked lovely—like the June roses blooming in the Gardens. We gave them their corsages, which they donned. They needed no enhancement, but it was sweet of them to accept our tokens. Babby took Rick aside. They didn't really know each other very well. Rufus went with them. He and Babby were old friends, after all. As I pinned on Jerry's boutonnière, he said, "You look great, Ollie. I'll marry you myself if the groom gets cold feet."

"He'd better not," I said. "Thanks, Jer, for everything."

"You two need to do something," Jerry said. "You need to take a trip. It's too late for Niagara Falls. The knot will be tied soon. But I think you should let Rufus stay with me for a week or so. And Jerome, of course. I can take some time off, and Betina can maybe look in on them when I have to work. You two should go someplace really boring. I've got it!" Jerry said with a great finger snap. "Bermuda! A soft bed, room service, and you can look out the window at pink sands if you need a change of scenery. I'll book it right after the ceremony. It'll be my wedding gift."

I was floored. I said, "Jerry, you have astounded me for . . . how many years? Thank you! But let's talk about this later. First, I have to get hitched." Prissy asked us to follow her to the spot where she would perform the ceremony. It wasn't a rehearsal, exactly. She just suggested where we should stand and what we should expect. Rick and I gave Rufus our rings. He said he was sure he knew which one he put in which pocket. I was just as sure as he was that he'd get it right, when the time came to produce them.

Guests began to arrive. I was delighted to see Will and Sam, of course. Sam had grown so much in the less than six months since I'd last seen him that I was quite amazed. And he looked even more like Will than when we first met. Sam and Rufus greeted each other. Sort of nonverbally, as kids do. I doubt I was ever that young. Will embraced me. He said, "You've been hiding Rick from me. I want to meet him."

"Of course," I said, and I led him to where Rick was greeting a colleague from school. "Will Granger, Rick Kashani," I said. I'll admit I was a bit tense about the prospect of the two of them sizing each other up. They were cordial, of course. That's what wedding days are about. They also seemed to enjoy the meeting. I relaxed, a bit.

They exchanged some easy small talk. Will and Rick were so very different, and yet, as I looked at them talking together, I realized they were equally precious—though Rick had earned the larger part of my heart, of course. Will said to me, "Let me find Sam, so we can figure out where we'll stand—or sit? Which is it?"

"There are some chairs in that little meadow right over there," I said. "Will, I'm so glad you're here."

"So am I," he said. "Let's talk at the reception."

I invented a reason to take Rick away from his teacher friends. "So, what do you think?" I asked.

"About?"

"About Will, of course. Please don't torture me, darling. Not on our wedding day."

"I think Will is every bit as attractive as you told me he is. Probably more so. I could work up a big case of jealousy, if I were so inclined. But I'm not. And the main reason I won't go there is that Will and I are now brothers."

"What?"

"We're fellow members of an elite band: Men Who Love Oliver Hartmann. Along with Jerry, of course."

"Jesus, Rick!" I said. "You're going to kill me before we get to 'I do!' "

"Speaking of brothers," Rick said, "another one just arrived." Sure enough, Carlos had entered the gardens and was working his way around the circular pathway that led to our little beachhead. Carlos was not alone, I was pleased to see. Marcus was with him. The two of them looked like a perfect wedding couple. Rick and I greeted them.

"We could make this a double ceremony, you know," I said. They laughed. Marcus went with Rick to meet some of his new friends.

Carlos looked at me very sweetly and said, "If you bring Rick half the joy you've brought me, then he'll be a fortunate man."

"Jesus, Carly! Everyone seems to be ganging up on me today," I said.

Carlos embraced me. He said, "Hush, Ollie. You can handle the good just as well as you can handle the bad. Don't stop now."

I pulled myself together. "Go, find Marcus," I said. "And don't fuck that up!" Carlos shot me his wonderful grin, and he strode into the June sunlight like a young god who's accepted a posting among mortals—as indeed he was.

The McNamaras showed up. I assumed they would. Joan's husband, Alex, looked the perfect mate for her—tall, fair, very handsome indeed. I liked him immediately. He said, "Oliver, I'm so glad we're finally meeting. My family is very fond of your family, and it's generous of you to include us today."

"Not at all, Alex," I said. "Thanks for coming." Aunt Cynthia and Uncle Charles were the last to arrive. I kissed Cynthia. I shook Charles's hand. I even managed a weak smile as I looked him in the eye for the first time in years. "I hoped you'd come," I said to them both.

"Yes, well, as you said, Oliver, we haven't much family," Cynthia said. "How is the child?"

"Rufus is great," I said. "Let me find him. He'll want to see you." I had coached him, of course. I told him to expect them to show up for the wedding. And I reminded him they were responsible for his education. He got it. I wasn't worried. He'd do well— as always. I was a little bit on edge about their meeting Rick. I found Rufus and asked him to greet them. He headed in their direction. And I went to Rick.

"Darling, Scarsdale is here," I said. "I hate to do this to you, but I'd like you to meet them."

"Of course, Ollie," Rick said. "You think I don't have dragons in my family, too? Let's get this done." We headed to where Rufus was charming his great-aunt and uncle. I could swear I saw Cynthia smile. A rare occurrence, surely. I couldn't help thinking that Rufus would be able to go back to school in September. And, after all, that was the important thing. I relaxed a little.

I presented Rick to my relations. Charles offered his hand, and Rick shook it. Cynthia offered her (gloved) hand, and Rick shook it. So far so good. It was all very polite. Rick said, "I'm so pleased you're here today. It means a great deal to Oliver, and to me."

Cynthia said, "Oliver reminded me how small our family has become, and, well, it seemed the thing to do."

"But it's more than that," Rick said. "You see, my *own* family declined to attend. They're in DC. They have other responsibilities. But my point is, *they're* not here today, and *you* are. And we'll always remember your support." *Shit!* I thought. *I'm way out of my league here. How will I ever live up to Rick's example?*

With everyone accounted for, it was time to do the deed. Rick and I suggested that the guests choose a place to sit. The celebrants were ready. "How do you feel, darling?" I asked Rick.

"Happier than I can tell you," he said.

"Let's keep it that way," I said. I reached for his hand. Prissy headed up the aisle and took her position. Rick and I walked forward, with Jerry and Babby following just behind us. Rufus brought up the rear of our procession. I'm willing to swear there was birdsong in the air. We took our places. It was time.

"Dearly beloved," Priscilla began. I was so pleased she started our ceremony with an archaic form of address that always felt just right to me. Yes, everyone assembled was dearly beloved (except for Uncle Charles, of course. But I even made an exception for him because it was my wedding day.) Yes, they were all dearly beloved, but none so much as the glorious man who had agreed to bind his life to mine. I looked at him. Rick returned my smile. And a sense of joy washed over me like a tidal wave. Yes. My *most* dearly beloved was holding my hand.

The End

This is a first edition from
Audacity Books
Please visit us on the web at
www.audacitybooks.com
For information, please send your request to
info@audacitybooks.com.

LOVE OBSESSED is Volume 3 of Bruce K Beck's **Obsession Trilogy**. *OPERA OBSESSED* is Volume 2, and *INK OBSESSED* is Volume 1. Look for *THIS IS GOD'S COUNTRY*, Volume 1 of the **Tolerance Trilogy**. And the **Love Trilogy:** Volume 1, *YOU'RE SURE TO FALL IN LOVE*, is set in Provincetown, MA, in the summer of 1976. *LOVE AND THE EPIDEMIC*, set in New York City in 1986, is Volume 2. Volume 3, *AND LOVE ENDURES*, is set in the early 1990s. For updates, and for occasional gifts and offers, please subscribe at:

www.audacitybooks.com/#subscribe

Many thanks to Walter Maas for his generous wisdom. And to Richard Kutner for his classy edits. I turned to Randee Sigal for her help with legal matters concerning custody and adoption. Many thanks for her expert guidance! Tim Barber of Dissect Designs (www.dissectdesigns.com) signed on as a cover designer for my first novel, and then became a friend. You're Sure to Fall in Love, indeed. This journey would not have been possible without the example and the teaching of Joanna Penn at www.thecreativepenn.com. I am delighted, Joanna, to add this volume to your long list of books you have enabled. No doubt you will hit your one million mark any day now!

Bruce K Beck is both a writer and an accomplished chef. His novels, including the **Love Trilogy,** the **Obsession Trilogy**, and ***THIS IS GOD'S COUNTRY* (Volume I** of the **Tolerance Trilogy)**; are available online and wherever books are sold. Before turning to fiction, Beck authored ***PRODUCE: A FRUIT AND VEGETABLE LOVERS' GUIDE***, which was called "gorgeous" by ***The New York Times***, "a dazzler" by ***Bon Appetit***, and "the most spectacular food book of the year" by ***The Boston Globe***. His next book was ***THE OFFICIAL FULTON FISH MARKET COOKBOOK***, which was called "invaluable" by Jacques Pépin, and "a treasure" by Irene Sax of ***Newsday***. And Rex Reed said, ". . . you'll love this book. It's like a movie!"